THE MYSTERY OF THE GOLDEN CAT

TAM MAY

The Mystery of the Golden Cat

Adele Gossling Mysteries: Book 4

Tam May

Published by Dreambook Press.

Click or visit:
https://www.tammayauthor.com

Cover Design © 2023 by Aries/100 Covers

ISBN: 9781734671407 (Print)
ISBN: 9781734671414 (ebook)

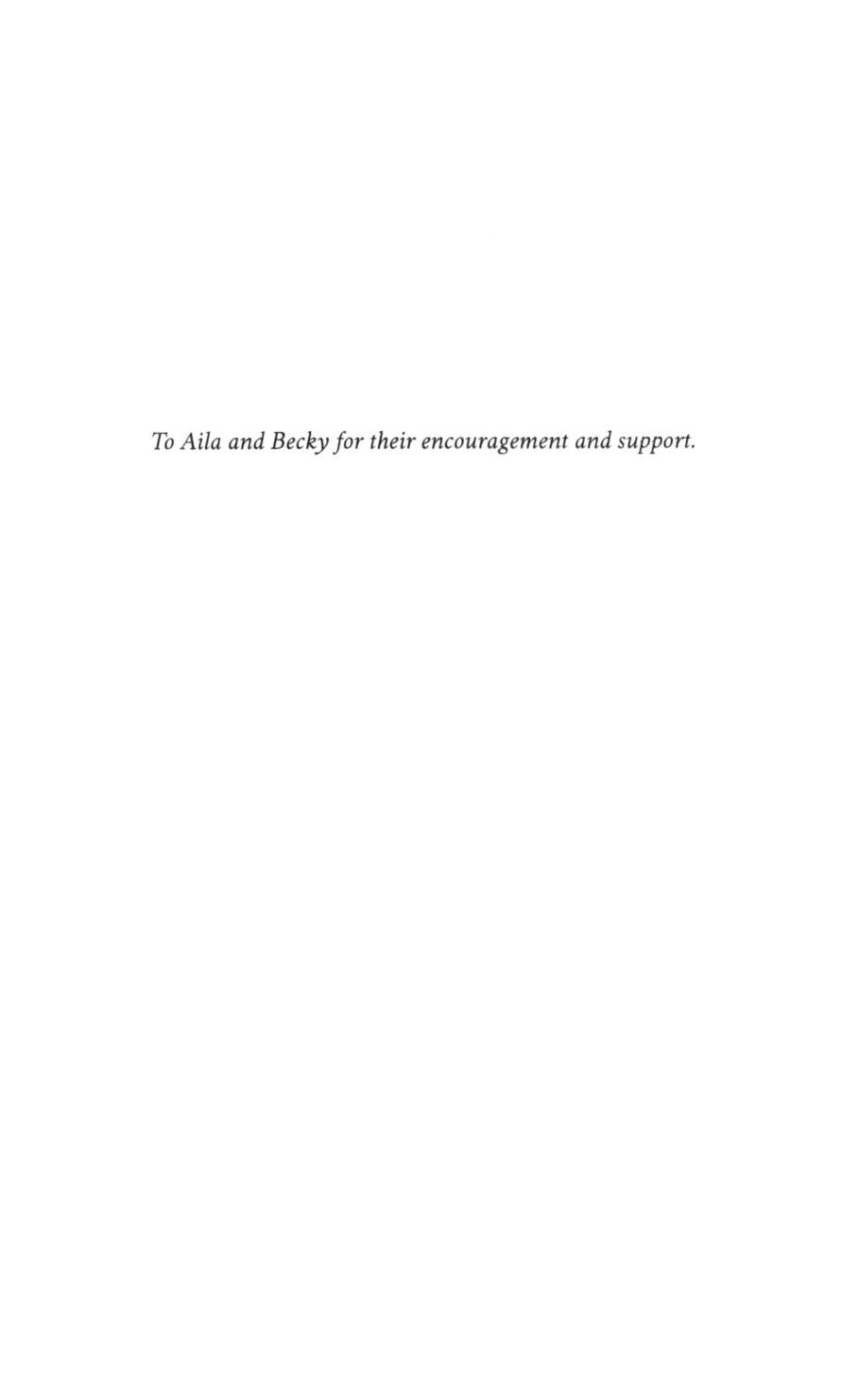

To Aila and Becky for their encouragement and support.

THE MYSTERY OF THE GOLDEN CAT

If you're interested in reading more early 20th century mysteries, my free offer at the end of this book is for you! So don't forget to check that out when you get to the end. Happy reading!

"You realize business people in Arrojo are taking Labor Day seriously this year, don't you, Del?"

The words greeted Adele with her coffee on the steamy September morning. Her brother Jackson bent over his sloppy oatmeal, as was his usual custom. He ate it without dropping any from his spoon on his starched shirt and jacket, the silk handkerchief tucked in his pocket in a perfect diamond shape. The deputy sheriff had impressed everyone in Arrojo with his immaculate appearance in the two years since he had accepted the position in their town, especially considering the sheriff could sometimes be a little too loose with his dress and even appear dingy and unrefined after a harrowing encounter with a criminal.

"I'm surprised you know it." She glanced at him over the rim of her cup. "I would hardly put the police under the heading of 'commerce.'"

"The town council informed us of the fact yesterday," Jackson said dryly.

"You mean Mrs. Faderman?" She put her fork down, the eggs sliding near the edge of the plate. Tomas, their hired man who insisted on acting as a footman as well, jumped forward with a napkin in his hand, ready to rescue the falling food, but it stayed inside the plate.

"And others," he answered.

"I thought the woman considered commercial enterprise little better than swimming in a hellhole," Adele remarked.

"Such language, dear sister!"

"But it's true, isn't it?"

"Apparently not this Labor Day," he said. "She and Mr. Raleigh and several others were most emphatic on the subject." Jackson shook out his paper.

"I'm anxious to hear what the good woman had to say," Adele said.

"Only that it's our civic duty and civic pride not to interfere with the shops this year," he said.

"Why this year in particular?"

"She didn't say," he said. "Neither did the others." He leaned forward and lowered his voice in mock confidence. "But I heard tell the last several summers have been slim for Bridge Street merchants and they don't want to make the same mistake this year."

"Their devotion to the holiday has nothing to do with an appreciation for workers' rights, then?" She eyed him.

"Hardly." He chuckled. "Mr. Raleigh confided in me —"

"Confided!" Adele snorted.

" — that most of the businesses in town have lost money most during of the summer so they'll need to rely on the visitors coming to the country over the holiday to help them pull through the year," he said. "I expect you shall too, though I imagine one can only sell so much, holiday or not."

"You talk as if I were just a paper peddler," she grumbled.

"Heaven forbid." He gave her an exaggerated bow. "Even Mr. Raleigh admitted your wares far exceed anything he offers."

"Then why hasn't he gotten rid of his stationery section?" Adele raised an eyebrow.

"Because, dear sister, there is something in this country we all appreciate," he said airily. "It's called a free market."

"There isn't much of that in Arrojo," she admitted.

"Ah, but there will be on Monday," he said. "Hatfield is expecting large crowds of people from the city."

Adele couldn't help but recall the colorful stories she had read in the *San Francisco Chronicle* growing up about holiday excursions to the country. *Hence, with air filling up their lungs and sunshine widening their hearts, carriages flock to the country roads from San Francisco to Sacramento like obedient ducklings, stopping in "quaint" and "untainted" towns. Neither are these thrill-seekers disappointed, as they ultimately return home, their arms filled with the best Vallejo and Creston and others have to offer. Or so the country merchants have them believing...*

"I can hardly wait," she said dryly. "You've been well informed about this town's commercial prospects, Jack."

"The police must always be informed of the quirks and habits of its citizens," said Jackson, without looking up from his paper.

She eyed him. "In other words, the council had a meeting yesterday evening."

"The sheriff attended that, not me," he said.

"And Mrs. Faderman made her pretty speech about commercial enterprise," Adele guessed. "Remarkable, considering the woman never owned a shop in her life."

Jackson sighed. "She loves to put her fingers into every pie.

3

Even those she demoralizes one minute while praising them the next."

She slid a triangle of toast out of the rack but held it suspended over her plate for a moment. "For the people north of Bridge Street, Labor Day is a celebration of their rights," she mused. "For Bridge Street merchants, it's a chance to make money."

"Well, why not?" Jackson asked. "For Father, it was a chance to people-watch at the picnic in Golden Gate Park. He ogled them like one would a bloody accident."

Adele gave him a sharp look. "It wasn't as shameful as you make it seem, Jack. People expect to be watched at a public park on a holiday."

"But not peered at under a magnifying glass." His face remained tight as he glanced at the hoop-shaped tool now hanging from Adele's throat on a gold chain. "At least you use it as it was meant to be used."

Adele fingered the trinket. "So did Papa. He was just as much a student of human nature as I am."

"Those men he defended were certainly prime specimens of human nature." Her brother growled. Thomas' eyes grew large with worry, always afraid of any harsh words between brother and sister.

"You always put people into little boxes, don't you, Jack?" she asked evenly. "It's not that easy for some of us."

"I wouldn't be much of a policeman without knowing that, Del," he snapped.

"Perhaps you're a good policeman in spite of it," she murmured.

Ruth poked her head through the door and announced the arrival of Hatfield. The sheriff nearly hit his head on the door-frame as he came out, his arms brushing against its wooden barriers. Adele had seen people jump at the sight of the massive figure with his badge shining in their eyes, but she knew his manner was always gracious, his voice soft-toned by nature and his smile amiable.

"You're just in time, Sheriff," said Jackson. "We were arguing about the law."

"Oh?"

The stormy feeling disappeared. "Jack was just telling me about Arrojo's sudden love of commerce. A rather progressive idea for the twentieth century." She grinned as Tomas scrambled to find Hatfield a chair.

"Yes, this town rather resists progress, doesn't it?" said the sheriff. His usual whimsical tone had a definitive edge.

"I wouldn't say Arrojo resists progress exactly," she argued, "but it certainly is selective of it." She dropped a lump of sugar in her small cup.

"Del thinks Arrojo limped into the new century rather than embraced it like she has." Jackson shifted his newspaper to rest on his other knee. "I told her about the town council meeting. I thought, with her shop, she ought to know what to expect on Monday."

"And it didn't change your mind?" Hatfield regarded her with interest.

"If they can't care much about the rights of workers," Adele remarked, "they have no business embracing consumerism in their own backyards."

The sheriff gave a deep laugh and plunked his hat down on the table. "Don't be too sure, Adele. Mrs. Faderman and the council may encourage commercial enterprise when it suits them, but they can still hold their own with the 'see no evil, hear no evil, speak no evil' crowd."

"I don't think I understand." She stared at him.

Hatfield glanced at her brother as Tomas laid another cup and saucer on the table as well as a plate twice the size of Adele's in front of him. "You didn't tell your sister the rest of the story."

"You said it was confidential, sir," said Jackson in a stiff tone.

"You know I don't make exceptions for Del, even if she is my sister."

"*I* make exceptions for her," Hatfield declared. "She's earned the exception with her help in three murder cases."

It was clear her brother did not agree, and Adele tried to hide her smile at the crease of annoyance on his forehead.

"And, er, may I say you look rather fetching in that yellow dress?" The sheriff sounded almost like a schoolboy.

"Thank you, Sheriff," she said. "But the color isn't yellow, you know. It's pale gold."

"Whatever you call it, it looks delightful on you."

Her brother cleared his throat. "I assume we're duty bound —"

"The council doesn't make decisions about the laws in this county, Jackson." Hatfield's voice was brisk. "I do."

Adele poured him more coffee and pushed the sugar bowl toward him. "You make it sound as if the town council believes the laws don't apply to them."

"They may be fools Adele, but they're not criminals," said the sheriff. "Though their behavior borders on negligence at times." This remark made Tomas stiffen.

"It must have been quite serious if it has you buzzing, Sheriff," said Adele. "You're usually more diplomatic than that."

"When we tell you about it, you'll see why I'm buzzing," Hatfield said. "I'm sure your brother told you about the reports we've received from my friend Sheriff Hill about thefts they've had in Sacramento."

"But that's far away from here."

"Not far enough, Del." Jackson folded the paper on the crease and laid it down. "Last week, we had a few thefts in some of the towns in this county."

"Vargas was the first," Hatfield said. "And yesterday, we received a dispatch from Wells Fargo that Rosa Gris and Blue Springs reported items missing from some of their shops."

"That's ghastly!" Her cup dropped to the table, missing the saucer. Tomas mumbled his dismay in soft Spanish. "No one was hurt, I hope?"

"The thief is only interested in valuables, not people," said Jackson. "There have been no reports of violence."

"Still — it's horrible to think —" She took another slice of toast from the holder, feeling her hand shaking.

Hatfield drew his hand toward the edge of the table between them. Adele's shoulders gave a quick flinch, though she knew the sheriff would never take liberties. But there was something in the man's gaze, his mouth closed but his eyes large and almost innocent, that gave her the sudden feeling of being in a too intimate corner with him just then.

"Perhaps Nin and I should warn the Bridge Street merchants before Monday," she suggested. "From one shop owner to another."

Silence buzzed around her, muting the brilliant blue sky to gray. Even the pair of doves nesting on the gazebo hushed up their morning song.

"We'll be very discreet, of course," she continued, her voice less assured. "We'll ask to speak to them in private."

The sheriff cleared his throat. "I'm afraid you can't do that, Adele."

"Why can't we?"

"Because," Hatfield said, "the town council refused to allow it when I suggested it."

"Refused!"

"They want us to keep it quiet, Del," said her brother. "We shouldn't have even told you."

The butter knife slipped from her hand and scraped against her empty plate. Tomas darted forward, mumbling in Spanish, glancing around to see if anything was broken. "That's perfectly ridiculous! Why, for heaven's sake?"

"They believe it would cause 'unnecessary panic' and 'soil the potential prospects for prosperity in our good town,'" Hatfield grumbled. "Those were Mrs. Faderman's words. They all agreed with her, of course."

"They had little choice," Jackson remarked.

Adele threw down her napkin. "So that's what you meant when you said their behavior borders on negligence! That civic pride of hers has blinded her again!"

"Not to mention made her deaf and dumb," Hatfield said dryly.

Adele rose, pacing the veranda. "Her behavior doesn't border on the negligent, Sheriff. It *is* negligent. Even criminal!"

"Really, Del," her brother mumbled. "Must you always exaggerate?"

"What else would you call it, Jack?" she insisted. "She's prepared to risk what could be a mess of thieves roaming in our midst."

"There's no evidence there's more than one thief," Hatfield said in a quiet voice.

"Well, Mrs. Faderman may be prepared to take that risk, but I'm not!" She threw a napkin across the veranda where it landed a few feet away from the steps. Tomas walked over and picked it up, shaking his head and mumbling.

"I was hoping you'd grown out of throwing tantrums." Jackson's voice was mild, but his curling knuckles betrayed his agitation. "This is quite unladylike of you."

"I promise you the other shop owners wouldn't want to take that risk either." She turned to Hatfield. "I understand you're under an obligation to honor their decision. But I'm under no such obligation and neither is Nin."

There was a heaviness in the air. "I told you we shouldn't have told her, Sheriff," Jackson barked.

She glared at him. "On the contrary. I'm glad you did."

"Ever since the Blackstone case, you think you have a license to involve yourself in all police business." He glared at her with defiance.

"And I've done just as well as you and the sheriff," she defended. "Nin and I have saved innocent people from the hangman and sought justice for victims who deserved it."

"I'm not so sure they all deserved it," Hatfield said, his voice still subdued. "Millie Gibb, for instance."

"That's not the point," Jackson said. "It's not fitting to a woman in your position, Del. Or in Miss Branch's either."

"You sound like Mrs. Faderman, Jack." She looked away.

"There are some things in which she's right." Her brother cleared his throat. "People are afraid to talk to me because of what you'll make of it."

"Oh, poppycock!"

"It's true, Del." He leaned forward. "How do you expect me to do my job if people are afraid you'll convince me of making a criminal case out of everything?"

"So you want me to keep silent just because I'm a woman." She lifted her chin. "You want me to follow orders and let the men with the silver stars handle everything. And botch it up, I might add!"

Hatfield's large elbows spanned the table. "I prefer to call it honoring their decision, just as you said."

"Call it what you like, Sheriff." She dropped into her chair again, pushing her plate away. "It still amounts to the same thing. You may be adding Arrojo to your list of robberies."

"Don't do anything foolhardy, Del." Jackson gave her a meaningful look.

"Is it foolhardy to want to protect my business and that of fellow business owners?"

"It is when you defy the sheriff's orders!" Her brother growled, and Tomas's brow wrinkled, his hands clasped at the sight of brother and sister fighting.

Adele turned to Hatfield. "You just said you determine the laws, Sheriff, not them."

"It's a sheriff's duty to go by what the majority feels."

"But you disapprove of the decision, don't you?"

The man stared into the backyard. His face darkened with the pallor of the gray. Adele realized he was watching the doves coo their morning song, sitting in their nest, trying to warm each other.

She spoke in a soft voice, "I'm sorry. Of course, if you tell me not to say a word about the thief, I'll keep my mouth shut."

He brushed his hand on the table. "The fellow may have moved on, and it's better not to cause unnecessary panic if he has."

She didn't believe Hatfield thought this, but she had enough reverence for him to curtail her temper. She emptied her coffee cup and rose. Tomas came forward at the signal to clear the breakfast table. "Let me tell Nin at least."

"I don't think that's wise, sir." Her brother's figure was stiff as the chair scraped behind him. "If we make one exception, we have to make a thousand."

"Miss Branch is no gossip, Jackson." Hatfield held the screen door open for her. "I see no reason to keep it from her."

"I'd feel better if at least two of us knew." Adele took the arm Jackson offered her, more as a gesture of peace for Tomas' sake, as she hated to see the distress on the kind-hearted man's face.

"Why would that matter?" her brother asked.

"Four eyes on a thief are better than two, Jack," she said. "And Nin's can cut sharper than a knife."

Hatfield laughed. "You mean six eyes. Ma intends to pay you a visit this morning."

Adele immediately felt warmed. Lady Augusta Hatfield was, despite her title, one of the most endearing figures in Arrojo. "That will be indeed a pleasure, Sheriff."

"She insisted upon it when she heard about the goings-on in Sacramento," said Hatfield.

"Then four of us will know about it," Jackson said in a dry voice. "Not very honorable of the council's decision, is it?"

"I think even Mrs. Faderman wouldn't object to Lady Augusta coming to my shop," Adele said. "Will she bring your father's 1848 Colt Dragoons with her?"

The sheriff smiled. "Both of them hidden under her skirts, I imagine."

Adele laughed. "I'll be flattered and honored to receive her." She sighed. "It's such a horrible thing to imagine there's a thief loose who can just walk away with anything he fancies."

"I doubt any thief would stand a chance against you, dear sister," Jackson said, grinning. "And certainly not Miss Branch."

She watched Jackson struggle with his gloves, absently marveling at how he always looked as refined as their father had riding the cable car to his law office every morning. An idea suddenly struck her. "Maybe you can give us some security, Sheriff."

"Interfering with police business again, Del?" Her brother gave her an arch look.

"You didn't complain when my interference, as you call it, helped catch Lucy Blackstone's killer," she shot back.

Hatfield peered at her from under the brim of his hat. "What sort of security, Adele?"

"I was thinking," she gave him a charming smile, "if you could spare Edison and the lads this morning, they might create a good distraction."

"What do you mean?" Jackson eyed her.

"Out of uniform, they're like any other young men mingling with the crowds," Adele said. "Except they'll be informed and they'll have their eyes and ears open and an assistant deputy badge in their pockets."

"I never heard anything so absurd!"

"Why is it absurd, Jack?" She glared at him.

"They're not trained to apprehend a criminal, sir." His voice rose with impatience. "They'll just be a flock of young men roaming the street, their eyes bulging like fish at the young ladies. That's hardly a way to catch a thief."

"I don't want to catch a thief," Adele insisted. "I want to keep one out."

"Jackson is right," said Hatfield in his mild way. "Edison is a good, sturdy officer, but he's young and a little feckless. The lads are even more so."

Adele looked from one to the other, clutching the handle of her parasol. "If Edison and a few assistant deputies dressed up in their Sunday best, everyone would think they were out enjoying the holiday, wouldn't they?"

Jackson gave a snort. "You've never seen Edison in his Sunday best, have you? He took the liberty of showing us the new outfit he bought for the picnic this afternoon. I daresay the others will be worse."

"Not everyone has your infallible taste, Jackson." Hatfield looked his deputy sheriff up and down in his dandified suit and chuckled. Jackson turned away.

"People are used to seeing them in town," Adele argued. "No one will think twice about it."

Jackson looked at his superior. "I thought you wanted them to go to Rosa Gris to help locate that swine Thornton."

"Wouldn't the possibility of preventing theft here in town take precedence over anything else?" Adele asked, giving the sheriff an innocent look.

"Now you're not only interfering, Del, you're impeding the wheels of justice." Her brother yanked his left glove up over his wrist.

"I'm doing no such thing!"

The sheriff said in a cautious tone, "I suppose it couldn't hurt to send a few of the lads down to Bridge Street, provided they go in pairs and we give them careful instructions."

"We don't exactly have the men —"

"From all reports, Thornton won't be going anywhere until after the holiday," Hatfield said. "If we can't warn the shop owners, we can at least provide them with some security, as your sister says."

"We would all be most grateful, Sheriff," Adele said, smiling sweetly.

Jackson remained silent for a moment, rubbing his stick with his hands. "Are you sure you're thinking of the shop owners, sir, and not — one particular shop owner?"

The sheriff's lips set with indignation, though his tone was good-natured enough. "I believe it's the right thing to do for all concerned, Jackson."

"I can't see Edison spotting a thief, much less catching one," Jackson lamented. "As Lady Augusta once said, he's not the brightest lantern in the stable."

"Perhaps not," the sheriff agreed, "but you can rely on him and the lads to give their best."

"Especially if you tell them it was my idea," Adele said slyly.

"All the more reason to send them to Rosa Gris," Jackson grunted.

"I believe the sheriff has the last word on this matter, Jack, not you."

That silenced her brother as he dug through his pocket, pulled out a handkerchief, and then, upon examination, rejected it, handing it to the waiting Tomas, who gave him a fresh one.

"I'm sorry I said that." She slipped a kiss on her brother's cheek. "Sometimes your prudence becomes too much even for me."

"And sometimes your lack of it becomes too much for *me*," he said. "I don't know how many times I've asked you to keep your nose out of things."

The sheriff gave a chuckle. "It's a little late for that, Jackson, at least where police matters are concerned."

As they stepped out of the house, Jackson said, "You realize they won't be inconspicuous to Mrs. Faderman and the other ladies. We may be in for some complaints."

"If they complain, I'll take full responsibility," Hatfield promised.

"I'm willing to tell her the idea was entirely mine," Adele offered.

He chuckled. "I don't fancy she would be very forgiving or forgetting if she knew that, Adele."

"I'm not afraid of her." Adele said with defiance as she strolled down the dusty walkway.

"You may not be," he said, "but *I* am."

Adele laughed as she pushed open the gate with her parasol. The sheriff had faced the roughness of the San Francisco docks and highwaymen on the Wells Fargo stagecoach. She doubted he would shirk from the gray-haired woman with the pince-nez who had appointed herself leader of Arrojo society.

~~~~~

On Monday, she saw her brother had not exaggerated. Businesses that usually opened their doors at nine or even nine-thirty were buzzing, though it was barely past eight. Shop windows were carefully arranged with grandiose displays, the shiny, white price tags facing the street. Painted signs stood in the sidewalks so she had to maneuver around them. As she crossed the street, she caught a glimpse in the distance of a wooden barricade where Ada's Millinery bordered the river. Adele had never seen Bridge Street closed off to wagons and bicycles before.

Her eyes fell on the darkened doorway next to her shop that belonged to Nin, her one staunch friend in Arrojo. The shutters were fitted tightly on the windows and she thought the young woman might be ill. Only yesterday Nin had complained about an upset stomach and had gone out to the wooded area not far from Adele's house to gather herbs for a soothing concoction, part of which she had given to Adele to keep on hand with strict instructions on how to use it.

Adele shoved the key inside the little side door in the alley between their shops and climbed the wooden stairs, the dampness of the narrow stairwell filling her lungs. She pounded on the entrance to the small flat where Nin lived over her store.

It took some time for her friend to answer, but Nin's head finally appeared, dark, lustrous curls tumbling around her face, her figure bundled in a colorful robe Adele knew had once belonged to her mother. Adele was relieved to see she looked freshly scrubbed without a sign of sickness or pain.

"I saw the closed shutters and thought —"

"I refuse to take part in this Labor Day bargaining," her friend growled.

"You're not coming down at all?"

"No one will miss me." There was a crushing note in her voice like a singing bird winding down in the twilight. Adele knew how much it pained Nin that some people in town still thought her a witch and feared her special gift of feeling auras and her knowledge of herbs, spices, and plants. "Not with all the strangers in town." Nin shuddered.

Adele took her hand. "That's why you've got to help me."

"You don't need my help."

"You're wrong, dear," she said. "I need your help today more than any other day." She then told her about the conversation that morning.

Nin was not surprised at the news of a thief. "I saw a dark cloud coming over the sun this morning. A rumbling of thunder, I thought. But the rest of the sky was blue." She looked into the window opposite. "That always means a warning from the Generous Ones."

"The worst of it is we can't tell anyone," Adele said. "I promised Jackson and the sheriff we wouldn't."

Her friend shrugged. "No one would believe us anyway."

She took the woman's hand. "I don't want to be left alone in my shop today." She felt a shiver wind its way down her spine.

Her friend leaned against the open door, a sharp look in her cat-like green eyes. "You really are afraid."

Adele stiffened. "I'm worried about losing money I can't afford, that's all."

"No, it's something else," said Nin in her far-off tone. "Intrusion. You can't tolerate that, can you, Adele?"

"Perhaps I can't," Adele admitted. "When one is used to being independent and an unwanted stranger puts his foot in the door —"

Nin gave her a wan smile. "The ladies might decide to put their feet in the door, and not to buy your wares."

"I don't think they'll interfere with my business now," Adele said. "They've accepted Adele's Stationers."

"Mrs. Faderman might still try to find another mark against you."

"I don't intend that she should." Adele was stubborn.

"You may be sure she'll put in the effort," her friend warned. "Today of all days. Holiday bargaining rates high on her list of civic duty."

"So I've been warned," Adele remarked, thinking of the sheriff's words.

"Don't worry," Nin assured her. "If she does, I'll be there to fight right alongside you. I shall be down in a few minutes, and I'll be properly dressed."

Adele pressed her cheek with a gloved finger and hurried down the stairs.

As promised, Nin appeared a few minutes later as Adele was removing the shutters. She had exchanged her usual wild woman appearance for a more socially presentable one. Her dark hair, usually free of pins and hat, lay tamed in a braid coiled in the back of her head and her dress, while of the flowing type she usually wore, looked unusually strained around her shapely figure. She wore short boots with tiny buttons, the likes of which Adele had never seen. Nin's loathing for shoes was well known in town and her bare feet frequently left their mark in the red dust.

"At the very least, Mrs. Faderman will have nothing to reproach me for in my appearance," Nin remarked as she helped Adele with the shutters.

Adele got into the spirit of the holiday commerce by attending to the displays of her best stock. She showed off the new colors of stationery that had just arrived from her distributor in San Francisco so that no one entering the door would miss them. She had Nin put the stamps in a pretty row near the counter and she arranged her most expensive pens and paper cutters on a table like a fan, so they caught the beam of sunlight streaming from the windows. She felt proud that their silver and gold shells gleamed with importance and attractiveness.

Her chest pounded as she saw Mrs. Faderman. The woman strolled with the measured steps of a bride going down the aisle, highly aware of the impression she left in the minds of those who greeted her. Her tall, stately figure breathed overabundant self-assurance. Adele stood in the doorway, watching the half-stillness of the street as shop owners and salesgirls peered from their windows, their anxious eyes on the woman as she examined the tables outside on which they had laid out their choicest wares.

"She wields more social power here than Mrs. Stanford and Mrs. Crocker do in San Francisco," she remarked to Nin.

And, indeed, it seemed the woman's sovereignty was so complete that everyone stood in attention, anticipating Mrs. Faderman's prediction of their success or failure on that Labor Day. Mrs. Faderman fingered a glass sculpture on the table outside Smithson's Gallery, inspecting it through the pince-nez always around her neck. Mr. Smithson cast a proud gaze on them as if waiting for confirmation of his worthiness.

"He looks as pompous as a peacock," Nin snorted. "Heaven help him if she frowns upon the gods."

Adele stepped away from her shop, catching a glimpse of Mrs. Faderman's decisive hands engulfed in kid gloves inspecting the glass sculpture. She found herself swept up in their anxiety. Would Mrs. Faderman give the item to the salesgirl to be wrapped or would she set it down on the table with a clatter and move on?

Mr. Smithson was to be blessed that day, for Mrs. Faderman jerked her head at the salesgirl. Mr. Smithson beamed and turned to hold out his arms to the street as if welcoming the crowd into his shop and, indeed, several entered its doors.

The Insworths, who owned the bookshop next to Smithson's, were not so fortunate. Mrs. Faderman fingered the pages of a book on the display rack outside, a copy of May Sinclair's *The Divine Fire*, frowned, and put it back. Cletus Insworth, who considered every book comparable to the Holy Grail, hung his head like a deflated balloon, and his sister Lucille slunk back into the shop as if she had failed the entire town in her duties.

"I see Miss Sinclair's latest book on art and love disturbs Mrs. Faderman," Adele remarked.

"Anything modern disturbs Mrs. Faderman," Nin mumbled.

The woman had crossed the street and was now heading toward her stationery shop. In spite of Adele's defiance of what society called "proper lady behavior," her hands grew damp and her fingers numbed. Seeing the way Mrs. Faderman's features stood with slack assurance of her position, the nervousness disappeared and Adele became determined not to let this woman's self-importance affect her as it had the others. But Mrs. Faderman seemed disinterested in her window displays, as her eyes fell on Nin's locked doorway. She stopped as if to take in the empty space and the tight shutters.

Her voice boomed with a shrill call, "Miss Branch!"

Adele winced. She had often seen the woman's sharp nostrils

flare with anger but not her temper. Her voice sailed out, "Good morning, Mrs. Faderman! Happy Labor Day!"

"Where is your friend, Miss Gossling?" The woman lifted the pince-nez to her fox-like eyes.

Adele tried to keep Nin back, but her friend slid past her, leaning against the display window. She waited like a child expecting a reprimand, eyes intent and lips unsmiling.

"Miss Branch, why is your door locked?"

Adele answered, "I asked Miss Branch to keep me company in my shop today. Wasn't it kind of her to agree?"

The woman pressed a fist into her hip. "Miss Branch, we've had this discussion before."

"We have this discussion every year," the dark-haired woman murmured. "Christmas and Easter."

"Your obstinance is unbearable!" The woman seemed uncaring that several of the townspeople were peering at them with blinking eyes.

"What you call obstinance, Mrs. Faderman, I call free will." Nin was undaunted.

"It won't be next year. We aim to make a city ordinance for every shop to be open on Labor Day."

"I'd like to see you try it," Nin sneered.

"Nin can't very well open her own shop if she's helping me in mine, can she?" Adele tried to sound cheerful.

The woman eyed her. "Why this sudden need for company, Miss Gossling?"

"You know why." Nin glared.

Adele could see Mrs. Faderman knew Nin was referring to the thefts, and her face grew a little less assured.

"Miss Branch, I ask you to reconsider." Mrs. Faderman's voice dropped a notch. "It's not very neighborly to close your shutters on a day like this, you know."

"But it's very neighborly to help one another," Adele pointed out, "especially on a day like this, when everyone's expecting a rush." She shielded her eyes and looked down the street where tubes of steam came from the direction of the train station. "The trains will run between San Francisco and Sacramento all day. People are getting off already."

"We must be prepared for them. *All* of us." Her hawk eye fell on Nin. "You've lived here long enough to know that, Miss Branch."

"And you've lived here long enough to know my shutters are always closed on a holiday," she snapped back. "Commerce or no commerce."

"I warned you last year I would have something to say about it if it happened again."

"And I warned *you* I didn't give a hoot about what you would say or do!" Nin growled.

"Perhaps you don't care what I say, but you may care about what I do," the woman said carefully.

Adele's eyes burned with anger. "What right have you to threaten my friend?"

"This is none of your concern, Miss Gossling," Mrs. Faderman said.

"It was her concern when you wanted her to persuade me to open my doors," Nin snarled.

Heads crowded the window at Raleigh's across the street and Mr. Crimson, who owned the toy shop next door, peered out his doorway.

"My concern right now is my shop, Mrs. Faderman." Adele's eyes sparkled. "So if you'll excuse us, we have work to do." She took a firm hold of Nin's arm.

The woman cast a meaningful eye across the street. "Mr. Starr has a larger place than yours, and he seems to manage with no help." She emphasized the last word.

"Mr. Starr has a pistol under the cash register," Adele remarked. "He's boasted often enough about knowing how to use it."

"What has that to do with it?"

"You know what, you old battle-ax!" This outburst startled even Adele, who was used to Nin's plain-spoken ways.

Adele had some satisfaction in seeing the woman jump, pressing her hand on her chest. She cleared her throat, speaking in a more complacent tone. "Of course, Miss Branch, if you're really helping Miss Gossling, I suppose that's all right."

"I'm glad you approve," Adele said dryly.

A procession comprising Edison, the lead assistant deputy, and three others appeared at the other end of Bridge Street. Adele understood now what Jackson meant about Edison's holiday attire. The young men were, as he predicted, about as inconspicuous as circus clowns. They wore almost identical tweed suits of black and red and derby hats too small for their heads.

At the same time, city people who had disembarked from the train filled the dusty sidewalks with their rustling skirts and felt hats. The carefully coordinated distance the assistant deputies kept between them quickly broke away in the confusion. Adele flinched as their squinting eyes scrutinized each person a little too fervently and their chins lifted with the overblown dignity of the important work they had been sent to do.

"Oh, Jack, I wish you hadn't been so on the mark," Adele murmured.

Mrs. Faderman's gloved hands clenched together to look like one enormous fist. "I assume you know what this is about?" It sounded more like an accusation than a question.

Adele leaned against the doorframe to steady her shaking knees. "I believe the sheriff mentioned something about a Labor Day patrol."

"You know I don't appreciate jokes, Miss Gossling," the woman snapped.

"I'm not joking, ma'am." She tried to keep the defiance out of her voice.

As Edison neared, he gave her a gloating smile, as if he had just won a game of cards. Mrs. Faderman grabbed the young man's arm and pulled him into the stationery shop.

"Mr. Edison, what is the meaning of this?" Her voice was shaking with panic and rage.

"Ma'am?"

"This buffoonish exhibition." She grabbed her pince-nez, which only made her eyes look more threatening.

Adele felt Nin's shaking figure behind her even before she heard her friend's soft laughter. She herself could barely hold back a smile at this unfortunate but accurate description.

"Why, ma'am, we're here to make sure there's no mischief." Edison's face turned an almost violet red as he stared at Adele. "We're here to protect the town!"

The soldier's pride in his voice made Adele feel a little ashamed of her laughter. She could see how right Hatfield had been when he said Edison and the lads would give it their best, despite their buffoonery.

"You'll do a fine job of it, I'm sure, Assistant Deputy." She patted his shoulder. The young man let out an embarrassed laugh, his face turning a more violet red.

"That's very admirable, Mr. Edison," said Mrs. Faderman, clearly affected by his words. "But what possible mischief could there be on a holiday?"

"You know what mischief." This came from Nin.

Mrs. Faderman ignored her. "We've never had any problems on Labor Day, and there's no reason to believe we will this year."

"Yes, ma'am," he said. "But we were told —"

"I'm sure you were told a great deal," Mrs. Faderman said, her eyes sliding toward Adele. "You were misinformed."

He looked at Adele with boyish helplessness.

"I think not, Mrs. Faderman," she said quietly.

"We would be pleased if you and your friends could take

yourselves off the street," Mrs. Faderman continued. "We'll see you all at the picnic later, of course."

Edison looked deflated as he mumbled, "If the sheriff says so —"

"*I* say so," she said. "You can tell the sheriff that."

"I hardly relish the thought of you as a sheriff in petticoats, Mrs. Faderman," Adele said dryly.

"The rest of us consider it a thought too horrific for your imaginations," Nin growled.

"Nevertheless —"

"Mr. Edison and the other young men are as concerned about the good name of Arrojo as you are," Adele insisted. "You wouldn't want them to go against the sheriff's orders, would you?"

"Is it the sheriff's orders, Mr. Edison?" The woman regarded the young man with sharp eyes.

"Yes, ma'am."

"We don't need deputies marching up and down the street, young man," she said. "It's extremely embarrassing."

The young man seemed genuinely confused. "Embarrassing?"

Her voice lowered. "Do you realize what would happen if our visitors knew you were the *police*? What would they think of us?"

Fury whirled inside Adele's head. "They would think we were looking out for their welfare."

The woman glared at her. "I don't see that's necessary, Miss Gossling."

"Of course it's necessary, you harpy!" Nin started for her again, but Adele held her back.

Edson looked at her, his face helpless for an explanation. Adele realized Hatfield had sent them to patrol without giving them the reason.

She leaned toward Mrs. Faderman and said in a soft tone, "Shall we let Assistant Deputy Edison get back to his job, ma'am?"

"I think not." The woman's regal calm held her in full self-possession. "For the last time, Mr. Edison, I ask you and those young men to leave Bridge Street. If you refuse, I'm afraid I have no choice but to pay a visit to the sheriff."

"As you wish, ma'am." He tipped his hat and strolled on, his hands behind his back and his walk wooden.

The woman pulled the collar of her jacket around her neck. "I believe I will tell the sheriff that young man is getting too impudent for his own good."

Adele's anger soared. "He's trying to do his duty."

"And for the right reasons," Nin added with a smirk.

The woman did not answer. She stepped out of the shop and snapped open her parasol.

Adele looked at her with anxious eyes. "You're not serious about going to the sheriff?"

"Naturally I am." She began down the sidewalk.

Adele ran after her even as Nin tried to pull her back. She lowered her voice. "We can speak plainly, can't we, Mrs. Faderman?"

"I haven't noticed you speaking subtly," the woman said, but it was clear from her attentive expression that she had every intention of listening.

"I think we ought to leave them undisturbed."

"But they're disturbing *me*," Mrs. Faderman said. "They're disturbing the businesses here." Her voice came down even lower than Adele's. "I don't know if you realize, but people here rely on Labor Day to make up for the slow summer months."

"I realize that," Adele said, "but if mischief ensues, it could be more costly than losing a few irate people."

The woman eyed her. "This is for you too, you know. You have your business, just like everyone else here. If Mr. Edison and those fops frighten customers away, they frighten them away from you as well. Now, I know you have other means of support, but I would hope you would think of them rather than yourself."

"Considering what might happen if the assistant deputies

leave, I believe having them stay is the lesser of two evils," Adele said stubbornly.

"What *might* happen," Mrs. Faderman said. "Why risk frightening people away from what could be the most lucrative day of the year for them because of what might happen?"

Adele's sympathy for the woman's stand turned into rage. "Arrojo isn't immune to tragedy, Mrs. Faderman," she said. "I should think what happened with Lucy Blackstone would remind you of that."

She immediately regretted mentioning the Blackstone case, as it had been a blot on Arrojo's respectable society. The woman's face went white as marble, and the parasol slipped to the side as if she were losing grip on it. But when she spoke, she was again self-possessed.

"I assure you I have no intention of speaking ill of Mr. Edison or the other young men to the sheriff. I simply want to get them off the street."

Adele studied her for a moment. The previous agitation was still on Mrs. Faderman's face, but she realized it came from the genuine concern for what the discernible presence of the police would do to Raleigh and Starr and others.

"Perhaps you're right, Mrs. Faderman," she admitted. "I shouldn't make decisions for others based on my situation."

"I'm glad you're beginning to see sense, Miss Gossling." The woman nodded with satisfaction.

Adele moved aside to let her pass. But just then, Lady Augusta Hatfield made her appearance in town. Her companion and housekeeper, Rowena, guided her wheelchair with a regality equal to her mistress.

"Good morning, ma'am!" Adele said over the soft murmur of the people on the street. The idea occurred to her that if anyone could detract the obstinate leader of the Arrojo community from her evil deed, it was Hatfield's mother.

She reached Lady Augusta before Mrs. Faderman. Out of

breath, she whispered, "We have to keep her away from the sheriff's office!"

Lady Augusta held up her gloved hand and winked. Rowena grinned and nodded in Adele's direction.

Mrs. Faderman now advanced, her lips spread with the smile of a perfect society lady. "What a pleasant surprise, Lady Augusta. We see so little of you in town."

"Not by choice, Irene, I assure you."

"Supporting our local businesses, I see."

"Indeed I am." Lady Augusta took up her position of authority immediately. "I came especially to see you. I need your advice, Irene."

Adele could barely contain her smile as she joined Nin in her shop.

As they entered, Adele could see the woman was so flattered, she was stumbling all over herself. "Well, I can't imagine what I could do, Lady Augusta, but you know I'm at your disposal." As she passed Nin, she hissed, "Do put that page cutter away, Miss Branch. You look as if you're about to cut someone's throat."

Nin's eyes sparkled, as if the idea appealed to her. Adele carefully removed the paper cutter from her friend's hands.

Mrs. Faderman cleared her throat. "What is it I can help you with, ma'am?"

"I'm here to find a gift for one of Horatio's cousins," the elderly woman continued. "A young man with great financial prospects who lives in some God-forsaken little town in Illinois."

"I'm sure Mr. Raleigh's store has several items suitable for a young man just starting out," she said. "And, of course, Mr. Starr's tailored coats —"

"I believe, ma'am," Rowena intervened, "you were looking for something a little showier than the average wares, weren't you, ma'am?"

Adele's glance fell on Mrs. Faderman, whose eyes were now seething with vexation. She bit back a grin.

"Mr. Raleigh's merchandise is hardly average, Miss Danvers." She spoke as if Rowena had no business knowing what Raleigh had to offer someone of Lady Augusta's stature in the first place.

"Rowena is right as usual, Irene," said her employer. "I'm looking for something — unique. I'd like to see what Miss Gossling has on offer. Her taste is always so discriminating."

"Thank you for the compliment, Lady Augusta." Adele bowed.

Mrs. Faderman's hand went to the edge of her hat. "I wouldn't confine myself to just one shop, Lady Augusta. There are so many bargains today."

"You ought to know by now, Irene, that when I set my mind to something, I set my mind to something." Lady Augusta gave her a steady look.

"I'd be happy to take you around the shops and see if we can't find something suitable for the young man." She leaned forward so the hanging pince-nez grazed the elderly woman's lap.

"Nothing of the kind," Lady Augusta insisted. "A young man like that is bound to need a few epistolary items. Isn't that so, Rowena?" She threw her head back.

"Indeed, ma'am." Her companion's tone was as severe as the dark suit she always wore. "More than a few, I'd say."

"Well, if you've made up your mind, you've made up your mind." Mrs. Faderman glanced at Adele. "You ought to be very grateful, Miss Gossling."

"I'm always grateful for Lady Augusta's patronage," Adele replied.

"You have some marvelous bargains for her, I'm sure?"

"You needn't worry," Nin growled. "She won't have to strain her eyes to find them."

Lady Augusta's lips twisted a little. "I've always had sharp eyes, Irene. From what my son tells me, we may need all the sharp eyes we can find today."

Mrs. Faderman's hostess look turned ashen. Adele couldn't help but feel a little sorry for this well-intended woman whose vision was perhaps skewed by her position in the community paired with her natural obstinacy.

"I think you ought to consider a visit to Raleigh's and Moffitt's, Lady Augusta," Adele said. "I saw some stunning cuff-links in the window of Starr's the other day that just might suit your nephew."

Mrs. Faderman's face lost the ashen look and, for the first time, she smiled at Adele with genuine gratitude. "If Lady Augusta prefers your shop, Miss Gossling, she'll be in good hands."

"I'm glad you'll be here to give her your expert opinion," Adele said, eyeing her.

"Naturally she will," said Lady Augusta with a pointed look. "I asked for your help, Irene, and I need it."

"She does have good taste." This grumble came from Nin.

"I have been told I have a discerning eye in all things." Mrs. Faderman smiled. "I suppose that other matter —" she glanced at Adele, " — can wait."

Adele took a quick breath. "If you'll follow me, ladies, I'm sure we can find something that will make your nephew's Illinois friends green with envy."

"Yes, yes." The elderly woman held her hand up to her companion. "Come, Rowena, and dear Irene." She said the last with a heavy gaze of her hooded eyes that was clearly meant to make any protest of Mrs. Faderman's disappear.

"She must be mad to want her along!" This came as a low cry from Nin directed at Adele's ear.

"She's trying to steer her away from exposing Mrs. Faderman's expert opinion to the sheriff," Adele whispered back.

"Scathing opinion, you mean," Nin snarled, and Adele giggled.

Lady Augusta took a deep breath. "Something about the scent of fresh paper makes me feel like writing. Doesn't it you, Irene?"

Adele's hands again grew damp as she watched Mrs. Faderman's appraising eye glance around her store.

"Certainly, certainly."

"Tea, Lady Augusta?" Nin jumped forward.

"Irene, would you?" she asked. "Nobody makes a strong cup of tea like you do."

"I thought my tea was fair," Nin murmured.

"Of course it is, dear," Adele said. "But Mrs. Faderman's tea parties are legendary."

The steel-haired woman gave her one of her brightest smiles and followed Nin to the front of the shop.

The moment she was gone, Lady Augusta took Adele's hand. "Now, dear, what is this all about?"

Adele recounted the conversation with Edison.

The elderly woman chuckled. "We came just in time, didn't we, Rowena?"

"Caught the gander in his tracks to save the goose," Rowena remarked in the way she had of odd phrases that always seemed right on target.

"She means well," Adele said.

The woman nodded. "Irene still has a little too much of that pioneering spirit."

"Blind faith it is," Rowena remarked.

"Don't you worry, my dear." Lady Augusta patted Adele's hand. "Irene may be stubborn, but she's not unreasonable."

Adele pressed the elderly woman's hand. "You're a true friend, Lady Augusta. In more ways than one." She added, "I know you came into town to draw people into my shop."

"And just how did you know that?"

"Your son told me this morning."

The woman's face dropped a little. "He's been so worried about these thefts lately that I hardly see him."

"He's committed to his work, ma'am."

Lady Augusta sighed. "Yes, Horatio commits himself to his work in the most honorable way, but I fear he's a little too committed. If it weren't for you-know-who —" Here she sniffed in the direction of the counter where Mrs. Faderman was making the tea. "She's always on him with her demands." She jerked her head back and called, "How's the tea coming along, dear?"

Mrs. Faderman rushed forward, balancing the cup and saucer with both hands. Adele caught sight of several Arrojo ladies who followed her around lingering on the sidewalk, glancing at the display window, trying to catch sight of Lady Augusta.

Nin was one step ahead of her. With a perfect curtsy that left her long, full skirt dragging on the floor, she called to them in a sweet voice, "Do come in, ladies."

The women shuddered with embarrassment but closed their parasols and mounted the steps.

"You do that curtsy so prettily, Miss Branch," Mrs. Faderman observed. "I'm happy to see you still have the manners of your affluent upbringing."

"Old habits seldom die, ma'am," said the dark-haired woman, "no matter how hard we try to kill them off." She slunk to her place behind the counter. Lady Augusta burst out laughing, and even Rowena chuckled.

But the steel-haired woman was clearly put out. "I can't see that good manners are as contentious as young ladies these days make them out to be."

"Good manners are like good intentions, ma'am," said Adele. "The results may be volatile even if the motive is pure."

Mrs. Faderman turned to Adele. "You seem to have been making quite a few insinuations about me today, Miss Gossling."

Adele bit her lip but recalled her father's words: *The shielded eye is not to be blamed for its blindness if there is a loving hand at work to open them.*

"You're right, Mrs. Faderman," she said softly. "I apologize."

"That's better." The woman nodded.

"I think it's time we laid all our cards on the table," Lady Augusta said. "We know about the thefts, Irene."

"We?" Mrs. Faderman glanced at the ladies.

"Adele and I," she said. "And Rowena, of course."

"And me." Nin's voice rose from behind Adele's shoulder.

Mrs. Faderman's face became grave. "I'm sorry you need to be exposed to such sordid details, Lady Augusta."

"I'm hardly innocent of 'sordid details' in my long life," the woman said. "Some of them happened in my own family."

Mrs. Faderman blushed and glanced at the shelf behind her.

"We also know about the meeting last night and your decision not to warn the others," the elderly woman continued.

"It wasn't *my* decision." Mrs. Faderman stiffened. "It was ours. The council's."

"I said lay *all* our cards on the table, didn't I?" Lady. Augusta's tone was razor sharp. "It was your decision, and everyone went along with it."

"I don't deny I have some influence in this town —"

"More than some, Mrs. Faderman," Adele said. "They were all waiting for you to arrive this morning, watching to see what you would buy and from whom. You've turned this day into punishment and reward with your civic pride."

"I've done no such thing!"

But it was clear the idea that she could have such sway over Bridge Street appealed to Mrs. Faderman. She could not hide the smug tilt of her lips.

"She looks like the cat that found the cream and licked it clean," Nin snarled in Adele's ear.

"Be that as it may, Irene," Lady Augusta's hands grasped the handles of her chair, "while we appreciate your reasons for keeping the thefts hushed up, we feel it was a mistake to do so."

"Hence the reason for Edison and the lads," Adele added.

"I'm afraid I can't agree with you, Lady Augusta." The woman stiffened, playing with the chain on her pince-nez. "I believe starting a panic when there's no reason for it would be the mistake."

"It's pure and simple selfishness!"

"Nin!" Adele gave her friend a cautious look. "Dear, see if you can entice the ladies to buy something. Please." Her pleading was so genuine that her friend's face looked distressed as she pressed her hand before scurrying over to the fluttering skirts near the front of the shop.

For the first time since Adele had come to live in Arrojo, Mrs. Faderman's well-measured dignity cracked. She looked almost ready to burst into tears.

"Nin shouldn't have said that," Adele said in a kind voice. "You've always had the interests of Arrojo at heart. We all know that."

"Thank you, Miss Gossling," the woman whispered.

Lady Augusta took her hand. "Since this is the day for bargains, will you go to Horatio with one?"

"Anything that will help me do my civic duty."

The elderly woman chuckled but went on in a firm voice, "Suggest to him that if he calls off Assistant Deputy Edison and the other young men, you'll consent to pass the news along about the thefts to the business owners and get them to keep it amongst themselves. I assure you he'll do it quietly, if only to encourage them to keep an eye out for any suspicious activity."

"If you'll pardon me, Lady Augusta, our local police haven't exactly been discreet, have they?" She glanced outside, where Edison was just passing, adjusting his bright red derby hat, and winced.

"I agree Edison could have worn more subtle colors," the woman chuckled. "But I'm talking about my son and Adele's brother, not about a score of eager but inexperienced assistants."

"I understand, ma'am."

"Will you at least think about it?"

"For the good of the community," Adele chimed in.

Mrs. Faderman stiffened. "I'll never shirk responsibility toward my community, Miss Gossling."

"All right then," said the elderly woman, though she sounded far from satisfied. "And now, Adele can show us some of her holiday sales."

"It was you who wished to see them, ma'am," said the woman. "I'm here merely as your guiding spirit."

A sound of incredulousness came from Rowena's direction. Lady Augusta gave her companion a fierce look.

The woman swept back the train of her skirt. "I have nothing I wish to buy."

The elderly woman eyed her. "You spoke earlier about supporting the businesses here. Don't you think it would only be fitting for you to be the first to support this one?"

Adele held her breath.

"Well, I —"

"Wouldn't you like Adele to show you some of her glass paperweights, for instance?"

"I have some lovely ones with California poppies," Adele chimed in.

"You need one, don't you, Irene?" Lady Augusta eyed her. "I seem to recall hearing about yours breaking last week."

Mrs. Faderman's cheeks flared like two red apples. "My maid, clumsy thing. I can't imagine how you came to hear of it." Her eyes slid with a seething look toward the front of the shop where Nin was helping Mrs. Abberton and Mrs. Cricket, the two women from her set whose tongues wagged worse than thirsty dogs.

Lady Augusta patted her hand. "Rowena told me, my dear. A wealth of information, Rowena."

Mrs. Faderman's silver head shone as red as her cheeks as she transferred the look to Lady Augusta's companion. She put the pince-nez on a little crooked and said in a brisk voice, "Miss Gossling, I insist we attend to Lady Augusta. Then you may show me the paperweights."

Almost immediately after Adele left Lady Augusta and her companion to examine the desk sets and Mrs. Faderman the paperweights, the rest of Mrs. Faderman's followers flocked through the shop. They examined the displays and called for assistance. Mrs. Lynn threaded her way between tables with her usual fluttery walk as if her shoes had wings. She asked in a timid voice, "Have you any cards, Miss Gossling?"

"Greeting cards, calling cards, or invitation cards?"

"Yes, that will do." Mrs. Lynn was always just a little vague.

As they walked, the feathers on her hat brushed against a row of rubber letter stamps. Adele rushed to keep them from falling.

"So sorry," the woman murmured.

A plump woman came sidling up beside them, her features similar to Mrs. Lynn's but more severe. "You remember my cousin, Mrs. Nitt?" Mrs. Lynn asked. "Cora, you remember Miss Gossling, don't you?"

"Certainly, certainly," Mrs. Nitt said in a brisk tone. "Last year, wasn't it?"

"Yes, when we had that horrible incident with the school-teacher," Mrs. Lynn said. "Oh, yes, quite a shock to all of us."

"So unfortunate." The woman sighed deeply.

"Miss Gossling is one of our more, well, forward-thinking young ladies."

Mrs. Nitt grabbed Adele's hand and pumped it with more vigor than necessary. "How dreadfully exciting! From San Francisco, as I recall?"

"Originally, yes," Adele said.

"Cora's daughter wants to study there," Mrs. Lynn supplied.

"Oh, they have so much culture in the city." The woman's bosom heaved. "Red Gulch is so backward in that area. But San Francisco, oh! The Paris of the West, they call her."

Her loud voice drew Mrs. Faderman. Mrs. Lynn stiffened with attention like a soldier in the presence of a superior officer. Her cousin went rigid too, her face freezing like a startled bird.

"I can't agree with you, ma'am," Mrs. Faderman declared.

"Oh, indeed?"

"People from the Middle West rarely understand the city." Mrs. Faderman spoke as if to a child.

"Irene doesn't like the city," Mrs. Lynn said quickly.

"You don't like San Francisco, ma'am?" Mrs. Nitt's face fell.

"The country is cleaner, both in place and spirit." She fingered the greeting cards on the table. "It's why my ancestors settled here."

"Oh, Irene, you're just a country girl at heart," Mrs. Lynn gushed.

Adele tried not to smile at the vision of Mrs. Faderman in a gingham dress milking a cow.

"That wasn't quite what I meant, Carolyn."

"But the city has so many opportunities for young people, don't you think?" Mrs. Nitt peered at her with hope in her eyes.

Mrs. Faderman gave her a sharp look. "For a young man, perhaps."

Adele knew Mrs. Faderman was about to launch into a lecture on the propriety of young ladies, one she made at every opportunity she could find. "Would you like to see my new engraved cards, Mrs. Nitt? They just came in last week." She reached for the drawer underneath the table.

The woman ignored her. "What about young ladies?"

"Some people might think so," said Mrs. Faderman, glancing at Adele. "I don't happen to be one of them."

"Why?" Mrs. Nitt's curiosity fired the word like a bullet, causing Mrs. Lynn to let out an embarrassed giggle.

"Because it gives them notions, dear." Mrs. Faderman used the same tone she had before.

"That's rather the point, isn't it, Irene?" Lady Augusta approached, a complete desk set resting in her lap. Rowena slipped up behind her, balancing an inkstand with two bottles.

"It might be, Lady Augusta, if those notions weren't so *questionable*."

"Things are so uncertain in big cities," Mrs. Lynn murmured

with a shrill laugh as she took a firm hold of her cousin's arm. "You were looking at the paperweights, Irene?"

But Mrs. Nitt's rather blunted mind seemed to get the better of her. "Whatever do you mean by *questionable* notions?"

"About their place in the world," Mrs. Faderman said. "Their purpose in life."

Adele had been biting her lip in an effort to hold back her retorts. It would not do, she knew, to argue with Mrs. Faderman in front of others when she had her business to think of. The ladies showed a genuine interest in the wares she had to offer. Nin darted around to keep up with calls for her assistance, and the pages in the sales book fluttered as she wrote out the slips. But Mrs. Faderman's insinuations stirred her temper.

"As one of the younger generation, may I speak?" she asked.

"You usually do, Miss Gossling, though you rarely ask permission," the silver-haired woman said dryly.

"We are in a new century," Adele pointed out. "Things are changing for women."

"And in some cases, not for the better," Mrs. Faderman insisted.

Ignoring this, Adele turned to Mrs. Nitt. "I think now is the time for women to explore their possibilities, especially young women like your daughter. And the city offers them so many."

She heard Nin chuckle with a certain amount of triumph, though her friend had as much disdain for the city as Mrs. Faderman.

"Oh, we have young ladies exploring their opportunities in Red Gulch too," Mrs. Nitt said in a knowing voice. "Those Gibson Girl types. They go around in their shirtwaists, riding bicycles and, I daresay, flirting with the young men a little too much."

"Precisely my point," Mrs. Faderman mumbled.

"Oh, but they're nice girls at heart." Mrs. Nitt looked frightened. "I didn't mean to imply —"

"Ma'am," said Mrs. Faderman, "I'm afraid you're being a little naïve." With a sweeping gesture, she bent down to inspect the card on the stand. "Perhaps you don't realize these same 'nice girls at heart' get ideas in their heads that quickly turn them arrogant and meddlesome in all the wrong places."

Adele felt her temper kicking up a storm, making her face hot and glowing. She was perhaps the only one in the shop who knew Mrs. Faderman was referring specifically to her involvement in some crimes that had occurred in town in the last few years.

"There isn't anything these days that doesn't concern women, young or not." She tried to sound calm.

The silver-haired woman regarded her with a caustic look. "I was referring to crime, Miss Gossling. Crime concerns *no* woman, young or old."

A series of gasps went through the little shop.

Mrs. Nitt shrank back as her cousin's face became soft and owl-like. "You don't mean —"

"Yes," said Mrs. Faderman. "Some modern young ladies even involve themselves in murder!"

A card fell to the floor, and Adele bent down to retrieve it. Her face safely hidden from the ladies, she let out a scowl.

"They're no worse than some not-so-young ladies who meddle in town affairs," Nin snarled.

Mrs. Faderman arranged her decisive countenance almost as a shield against the remark. "Crime is best left to the police, Miss Branch. Even to those who have influence with the police through family members or some other means."

Adele looked straight at Mrs. Faderman. Her acute eyes and defined cheekbones jolted out in indignation. She wondered if Mrs. Faderman suspected she had been the one who convinced Hatfield to send out that morning's patrol.

"My, but you're a suspicious character, Irene," Lady Augusta said in a dry voice.

"Stuff and nonsense." This sniffling affirmation came from Rowena.

Their eyes slid in Adele's direction, and even Nin was standing with her arms wrapped around the sales book, waiting for her response.

Adele was almost relieved when she heard agitated voices coming from further inside the shop. Excusing herself, she threaded her way around the displays until she reached two men arguing over a table, each holding one end of a rectangular box. She recognized one of them as Mr. Lyman, a clerk at the Arrojo Finance Company, looking rather dapper for the holiday in a spotted bow tie the color of his coat and spats. The other was a stranger, an older man in a suit well-made but wrinkled.

"It *is* a 1781 Nostrum!" the older man shouted.

"Nonsense," said Mr. Lyman. "The box clearly says Montache Special."

"Indeed," said the man. "One does not judge the immortality of a pen by the *box*."

"Why, you haven't even looked at it!" Mr. Lyman's voice resembled a dog whining at the moon. "I've been waiting for this pen to be reduced for some time. I need it for my work. You wouldn't deprive a man of his work tools, surely." He gave the box a tug in his direction.

The older man eyed Mr. Lyman's impeccable suit and bow tie. "Your work, young man, seems to have made a dandy of you."

Mr. Lyman's hand flew to his neck, but he seemed more concerned with the position of his tie than the older man's insult.

The other grinned, as if sensing he had hit his mark. "My reason for wanting this pen is far more important than yours, sir. I'm a collector of Revolutionary War relics. My great-great-grandfather fought —"

"Judging by your age, sir, I believe it should be great-grandfather," the young man said stiffly.

Adele put herself between them. "What's this all about, Mr. Lyman?"

"Miss Gossling." He seemed relieved. "I beg of you, please inform this man he hasn't stumbled upon an eighteenth-century memento. Maybe if he hears it from you, he'll behave in a more gentlemanly fashion."

"I beg your pardon, miss," said the man with a tip of his hat.

"I'm afraid Mr. Lyman is right," said Adele. "That pen came from the Montache company only a few weeks ago."

His manner shifted from cordiality to wariness. "Are you sure you didn't buy it at an auction and simply forgot about it?"

She eyed him. "I believe I know where my stock comes from, sir."

"I've yet to meet a shopkeeper who really knows the value of his or her wares," he said. "Especially when that shopkeeper is a woman, if you'll beg my pardon."

"How dare you insult Miss Gossling!" Mr. Lyman's outburst sounded so melodramatic that a chuckle rang through the women nearby who had stopped to listen to the argument.

"I assure you, a businesswoman is more aware of the value of her merchandise than a businessman," Adele snapped. "Perhaps you'll beg *my* pardon when I say the men who do business with her will always try to cheat her if she isn't."

"I mean no offense, miss." The man's tone was patient. "I know small-town shops often gather a variety of old and new things, which is why I like to haunt them for my relics."

"All the merchandise in my shop is modern," she said. "Perhaps you'd like to have another look at the pen you're so interested in buying." She nodded toward the now slightly smudged box. "I'm sure it will settle this matter once and for all. If Mr. Lyman would be so kind as to relinquish his half of it."

Mr. Lyman obliged, though clearly reluctantly. The older man opened the lid and his face was startled as he viewed the oval-shaped barrel with gold snakes twisted around it and a glaring stone in the center.

"Good lord, what a ghastly-looking thing!" He handed it back to Adele.

The exclamation caused another ripple of laughter.

"It's the latest model," the young man insisted.

"And exactly the taste of a young dandy like yourself," said the man as he handed it back to her.

"Then it's yours, Mr. Lyman." Adele put it in the young man's waiting hands. "If you'll come this way, I can ring it up for you."

The other man seemed reluctant to leave so soon as he trailed after them. "Perhaps you'll kindly tell me where I can find a good antique shop, if there is one in this town?"

"I suggest you try Ellingworth Antiques." Adele clicked the register. "Cash, Mr. Lyman? Mr. Lyman?"

The young man was looking through the doorway. The older man's gaze followed.

"Odd," Mr. Lyman murmured.

"Like chickens with their heads cut off," the other man agreed.

Their sudden attention pulled Adele away from the cash register. People were running through the street. Shrill cries escaped the ladies.

"Lord, I hope it isn't a fire," the man in the crumpled suit said. "Just my luck."

"Our fire laws are as good as anybody else's," Mr. Lyman sniffed. "Still, I wonder — help, a wild beast!"

Before Adele could ask for an explanation, he bolted out the door. The man in the wrinkled suit followed close at his heels.

People ran out of her store, scattering about. A feeling of dread filled Adele's chest as she imagined the thief, a sinister-looking person with half his face covered, perhaps a revolver in his hand. But when the dust had settled from the stomping feet, the man she saw standing in the street looked far from criminal. He was tall and dressed in evening clothes that had clearly not been washed or pressed for some time. In his hand he held a rope and at the end of that rope, sitting with rapt attention, was a tiger.

Adele felt her head spin.

"Are you alright?" She heard Nin behind her.

She closed her eyes for a moment, hearing the sound die down outside until there was absolute silence. When she opened her eyes again, the man was in front of her shop. Up close, the animal at the end of the rope was even more astounding. Its coat shone in red-gold streaks under the sunlight. When it opened its mouth to give a roar of greeting, its teeth looked nearly gold too.

She realized the man himself disturbed her as much as the animal. His eyes were uneven and his lips spread with a clownish smile. But it was not a cheerful smile.

He gave her a deep bow. "My golden cat would like to meet his golden queen. May we?"

The tiger threw its head back in reply, causing another stir in the street.

Adele's hand flew to her chest as she remembered Hatfield's compliment about her dress that morning. She felt as if she were gleaming in the sunlight, blinding all eyes that came upon her. She touched the magnifying glass, thinking of her father sitting in the parlor after dinner with his head bent over one of his books, the thing almost touching his eyelashes as he held it so close to read the fine print. The image calmed her.

The man repeated, "May we?" He was inside the door before she had a chance to respond.

Pandemonium broke loose on the street. The air filled with screeches and flapping arms like birds trapped in a closet. She whirled around, realizing the shop was empty besides herself, Nin, Lady Augusta, and Rowena.

"What is the meaning of this?" the elderly lady demanded.

Nin rushed forward. "Get out!" She kicked the man's ankle.

The tiger regarded her with a wary yawn that showed its golden teeth.

The ease in the man's voice matched his insincere smile. "There's no need to be alarmed, ladies."

Adele motioned for the women to get behind the counter. But Lady Augusta remained where she was, her head held high with the regality of her title, and Rowena stood behind her employer with equal courage. Nin, too, stayed where she was, though her hand grabbed the edge of the table behind her.

"Sir, I insist you leave immediately," Adele growled. "I won't allow that beast in my shop."

"I assure you, dear lady, Sinbad is as gentle as a kitten," said the man. "Especially in the presence of the fair sex."

"How terribly cultured of him," Nin snapped.

"Oh, indeed, miss, my cat is most cultured and most polite." He motioned toward the animal. "Bow to the ladies, Sinbad."

The tiger rose on its hind legs and made a gesture with his head that could pass for a bow. Adele heard a sigh escape her friend. Rowena sniffed but no longer looked alarmed. Only Lady Augusta was unimpressed.

"It's hardly civilized to roam around town with a wild beast," she said in an icy voice.

"And a strange one at that," Nin added.

"A golden tiger." The elderly woman nodded. "I've seen only one in my travels. They're very rare, I understand."

He burst out in a jovial laugh. "Exactly. And think of the publicity, noble woman. A mere orange cat is a common thing. But gold is the color of enchantment."

Adele now looked at the animal with pity. It gave a merciful yowl. "And what is your name?"

The grin on his face vanished, and he was suddenly all business as he presented her with a card: *Lionel Sipes, Entertainer, parties, galas, events.*

She handed it to Lady Augusta without taking her eyes off

Mr. Sipes. The elderly woman read it and snorted. "Entertainer! Charlatan is more like it."

"Drawing rings around his words," Rowena remarked.

"Nothing of the kind," he insisted. "I come from an honorable family."

"Well, Mr. Sipes," said Adele, almost completely recovered. "Now that you've scared away my customers on one of the busiest days of the year, perhaps you'll let me know why."

"I didn't intend to frighten anyone, dear lady."

"That's not true!"

The man looked annoyed, but Nin said this with the assurance Adele knew must come from one of her auras.

"I think that was precisely your intention," Adele said.

The eyes again sparkled. Adele noticed they were a mix of brown and green. From the sunlight that streamed through the shop, their hazel colored gave off a glittering yellow.

"But you're wrong." Mr. Sipes pulled the rope to bring Sinbad to his feet. "I only wanted to make an entrance."

"You made it all right," Lady Augusta said. "Just what sort of entertainer are you, Mr. Sipes?"

He began rattling away in a mechanical tone, "I've worked with some of the finest shows in the country, including The Palace in New York. I've traveled all over Europe and been admitted past the gates of some of the most lavish homes. I've entertained a sheik's harem —"

"I rather doubt that," Lady Augusta said, and her companion jerked her head in agreement.

He cleared his throat. "I've attended an emperor's garden party and a nobleman's court. I've wooed and dazzled the highest authorities, including the Queen of England—"

Nin interrupted him, "King. King of England."

"Oh, him too, him too," the man insisted. "Sinbad took quite a shining to the man. Why, he even ate an apple out of his hand."

As he spoke, the animal came to life. It rose with a low growl and examined the floor under tables, shelves on displays that it could reach, and even eyed the gleaming items through the glass in the front. Adele realized the rope allowed Sinbad to wander almost to the edge of her shop.

"I really don't think —" she began.

"Ah, but dear woman, you don't have to think because I *know*. I've been watching your establishment for some time, and I know only the finest people enter your doors. I will tell you in confidence —" He leaned so close she could see the uneven shave on his face. "I don't come with this proposition to everyone. Only the finest shops with the finest people can give away my services. For a small part of the profits, of course."

"What makes you think my customers would be interested in your kind of entertainment, Mr. Sipes?" She eyed him. "You saw how the people on the street reacted to you and your — cat."

"I rather think you enjoyed that," Lady Augusta remarked.

"Relished it," Nin agreed.

"Indeed not, dear lady," he said through his grin. "They were just people on the street. But fine people such as those who come to your store are fond of enlightened forms of entertainment."

"And just how is yours enlightening?"

"Sinbad will delight after-dinner guests and awe children with his tricks. What could be more enlivening than an intelligent, well-handled cat like Sinbad?"

"I wish you would stop calling it a cat!" Nin snarled.

"Mr. Sipes," Adele's voice rattled with anger, "my friend is right. Sinbad is not a cat but a wild beast."

"I'm simply trying to make a living."

"I don't think the police would find your cat as harmless as you do," she continued. "In fact, I don't think they would relish the idea of a wild animal roaming their streets."

"I've had no trouble so far," he said in a mild tone.

"You will with the Arrojo police," Lady Augusta spoke up. "My son, sir, is the sheriff of this town."

"And my brother is the deputy sheriff," Adele added.

The rope slipped from his hand and the tiger shot past Adele and disappeared around the shelves.

"Sinbad!" But Mr. Sipes' tone was more scolding than alarmed.

Nin pinned herself against the wall, and Rowena joined her behind the glass counter. Even Lady Augusta, whom Adele knew had seen wild animals during her hunting trips with Lord Hatfield, looked more than a little frightened.

"You did that on purpose!" Adele's hand grasped at the chain around her throat as if it were a lifeline.

"My dear lady, Sinbad is only curious," he said. "But you needn't worry."

"Perhaps you ought to teach it that curiosity does no good to a cat, as the saying goes." Lady Augusta glared at him.

"Call him back!" Nin said.

"Sinbad!"

"Mr. Sipes, I will not tolerate this!" Adele shouted.

A strangely hypnotic look replaced the previous clown face. His gaze made her feel more restless than the tiger now loose in her shop.

"I wish you would stop staring at me!"

"Too lovely, too lovely." His skin had turned tan and leathery, reminding her of the men she had seen on the streets in San Francisco with their faces worn from years of traveling on the road and sleeping out of doors.

"Sir, your impertinence is obscene," said Lady Augusta. "Call back the tiger and leave these young women alone."

"It isn't Adele he's looking at," Nin said.

Adele followed Mr. Sipes' eyes and saw they were level with the magnifying glass hanging around her neck. She shielded it with both her hands like a mother protecting a child.

"I am an admirer of such trinkets," he said as he took one step closer and held up his hand. "May I?"

"These are my friends, and I won't risk their lives," Adele said, ignoring the request. "If you won't go after Sinbad, I will."

"Adele!" Nin screeched.

"I don't think that's wise, my dear," Lady Augusta said in a softer voice. "Not without a pistol or a weapon of some sort, anyway."

"All right, then." She grabbed a long paper knife that had been moved aside on one of the tables in the earlier rush and held it in a stabbing position.

Mr. Sipes had not yet taken his eyes off the necklace. "You wouldn't do that to a friendly cat, dear lady. I'm sure of it."

"I would if it would end this sick game of yours."

He moved in closer to her. "We all play our little games, don't we?"

"We don't like yours, Mr. Sipes." Lady Augusta looked at him squarely.

"A terror all over the place," her companion Rowena declared.

"I'm merely interested in an ornament around the neck of a rather interesting young woman," he said.

"It's out of the question!" Lady Augusta snarled.

"I'd be obliged if the dear lady would answer for herself." His voice lowered a little. "Ah, she hesitates. Were it a mere trinket, I would have it in my hand."

Adele clutched tighter at both the necklace and the paper knife. "You think you have tremendous powers of observation, Mr. Sipes."

"One must, in my profession," he said as he took yet another step forward. "Entertainers must be keen to public disregard or approval. It may cost them their livelihood and even their lives in this wild country if they are not."

"Your fascination with my rather interesting ornament, as you call it, is exaggerated." But her voice shook. "It may be interesting and ornamental, but nothing more."

Mr. Sipes' voice was so low, it was almost soothing. "We both know that isn't true, don't we?"

Her hands shook as she drew them away from the magnifying glass. "Mr. Sipes, I'm warning you for the last time. Either you go after your cat or I will." She poised the knife like a dagger and began making her way toward the back of the shop.

He reached a hand toward her. "I wouldn't advise that, dear lady. Sinbad is partial to young women, but he can be unpredictable. Especially If he sees you with that." He looked amusingly at the paper knife.

Adele glared at him.

"I will gladly call Sinbad, and we will leave your charming place," he said with a quick bow. "After you've allowed me to examine your precious necklace."

"What cheek!" Lady Augusta's face turned white with outrage.

Adele's hand covered the magnifying glass. "Why are you so interested in it, Mr. Sipes?"

"Because it's clearly precious to you." His eyes met hers with surprising seriousness. "A lover's gift?"

Adele couldn't help but snort at this.

"A family heirloom, then," he said. "I am a great believer in family heirlooms."

"Can't you see you're upsetting this young woman?" Lady Augusta snapped.

"I'm not upset," Adele promised.

"You're not going to do it?" Nin nearly jumped on the glass counter.

"Mr. Sipes hasn't given me much choice, has he?" There were sounds of tumbling and pushing coming from the back of the shop.

She cupped the necklace in her hand, feeling the cold metal against her skin. She thought about her walks among the beautiful flowers of the conservatory at Golden Gate Park with her father, threading the crowds as Jackson held the parasol open above their heads. She saw her father with one hand behind his back while the other fingered the magnifying glass, bringing it to his eye, somewhat nearsighted from bending over books in his darkened law office. She could almost hear her father remarking on a strange quirk or sign deciphered through the glass.

Mr. Sipes watched her. "Don't be afraid, dear lady. I shall handle it with the greatest delicacy." He reached into his pocket. "Poor as I am, I know the value of a family heirloom."

The pocket watch looked much like the one Jackson had received from their father. Her brother, despite his immaculate habits, strangely neglected it and the watch had had to be repaired more than once. This watch, in contrast, was well taken care of. The hinges on the top showed it once had a gold lid that must have broken long ago, but the glass face was unscratched and polished in spite of this. Turning it over, Adele found an intricate pattern of two intertwined dragons. Between their weaved bodies was engraved, *To my son—with love and affection.*

"My grandfather gave my father this watch," Mr. Sipes said. "My father gave it to me."

"From father to son," Adele murmured.

"So you see, I appreciate sentimental objects, just as you do."

She was no longer reluctant to give him the necklace, and even the protests of the women around her ceased, except for Nin's. The knotted look on her friend's face showed more disturbance than it had at the sight of the loose tiger.

Mr. Sipes's manner became at once intense. He produced a loupe from his pocket and held the necklace close up as he examined it.

"Magnificent," he said. "Magnificent trinket. And yet, not entirely."

"Not entirely?" Adele raised her eyebrows.

He seemed not to have heard her. "It's a magnifying glass, you say?"

She nodded. "It's been of great use in helping the local police solve cases."

THE MYSTERY OF THE GOLDEN CAT

His fingers gently touched the leafy engravings on the outer shell of the gold medallion. Though he was keeping his promise to handle it delicately, his zealousness made her skin crawl.

His anxious eyes betrayed the casual flow of his voice. "Your father must have been a man of foresight."

"What do you mean by that?"

"Why, dear lady, isn't gold even more precious in these times?" His eyes were wide as an owl's.

"You said the value was sentimental." Nin peered at him.

"And so it is, dear woman. So it is."

"But you believe a family heirloom should have more market value than sentiment?" Adele asked.

"It's not what *I* believe, dear lady." His eyes grew dim in the small shop. "It's what the gold kings believe."

"There are others who believe we shall soon see silver take its place on the market," Lady Augusta said.

He smiled a little. "You speak rather knowledgeably about such worldly things for — if you'll beg my pardon — a woman of retiring age."

"I may be of a retiring age, sir," said the noble woman stiffly, "but I can still read a newspaper."

He let the necklace hang from his finger. It swung back and forth. "You think we oughtn't to despair, then?"

Clearly, the elderly woman was taken aback. "I never thought much about it."

That morning's argument came back to Adele, and she realized why Mr. Sipes' look disturbed her so much. Some of the men her father defended in the last years of his life had looked exactly like Mr. Sipes did now. Not so shabby, of course, but soap and water could not mask their hooded eyes and grim smiles. Their hate for the world showed in every gesture and every word. Mr. Sipes, however, had no skilled lawyer to help him camouflage his defects.

"You've had your look, Mr. Sipes?" Her voice was steady.

"Naturally, naturally."

"Then I'd be grateful if you would give me my precious heirloom back." She held out her hand.

"And then get your cat and get out," Nin growled. "Or I'll feed him ink and poison him!"

The spell was broken. The man burst out laughing. "Fair enough, dear lady. I hope you and your friend will come see my cat perform some of his tricks some time." He handed Adele back the magnifying glass. "Korba & Sons, is it not?"

"I don't know," Adele mumbled.

"I daresay she doesn't care," Lady Augusta said.

"The end is more worthy than the means." Rowena nodded with satisfaction.

"Korba & Sons." He said this with finality, as if settling the matter. "The Greeks know about the beauty of infinite things." He sighed then. "Such is gold, you know. More infinite than those who value it."

The tiger appeared then, making an odd noise that shook its body. It propped itself against the glass counter on its hind legs, looking at Nin with interest. She screeched and jumped back.

"Rowena," Lady Augusta said in a steady voice, "will you please run down to the police station and ask my son to come here immediately?"

The woman grabbed the edge of her skirt and clopped toward the door.

"Wait!" Mr. Sipes grabbed the rope, pulling Sinbad away from the counter and patted him on the head, whispering in his ear. The animal lay on the floor. The man looked at Nin with the clown smile. "Sinbad's taken quite a liking to you, dear lady. He only takes an interest in those he judges worthy of his company.

"Like the Queen of England?" she answered dryly.

Mr. Sipes let out a sharp whistle. The tiger rose, bumping into a small table where it upset a jar of pencils. "As you've been so kind, I beg of you to indulge me a little further. Please take some of my cards, as I'm sure your patrons would be interested." He dropped a handful near the cash register. "Hold on to your family heirlooms, dear ladies. The gold ones, that is." He tipped his pipe hat and disappeared down Bridge Street, pulling the tiger behind him.

The moment he was out of sight, Adele flung her hand across the stack of cards so they scattered all over the floor. "The impudence!"

"Don't worry, dear," Lady Augusta said in a soothing voice. "We shall go at once to Horatio and have the man thrown out of town."

Adele felt the crumbling sound of crepe skirts brush past her as Nin went to the doorway. Although her back was turned, Adele could feel her glassy stare, and she knew her friend had received one of the strange auras that flowed through her like an electrical current.

"The man is evil!" she declared.

Lady Augusta, who had been fiddling with packages in her lap, said in an off-hand way, "a charlatan, perhaps."

"No, no!" Nin pressed her hands together. "A boa constrictor."

"A rather apt description for a charlatan," Lady Augusta said with a chuckle. "Dear, will you ring up our things?"

Adele stared down at the cards the man had left, which Rowena had placed in a small stack near the pen and pencil holder. "I agree with Nin."

The woman leaned her head at her. "Because he dared tread on your sacred ground?"

Adele looked at her, feeling a sting in her eyes.

"He had no right to touch her magnifying glass!" Her friend came to her defense.

"Adele gave him that right," said Lady Augusta gently.

"He cornered me," Adele lamented.

"Yes, I suppose he did," the woman mused. "It's the way with charlatans. They pin people against the wall." Her head tilted.

"Did I ever tell you about the arrest of Frederick Merrimont, Rowena?"

"I don't suppose you breathed a word of it, ma'am," she said as she helped Nin place the desk set in a box.

"It isn't a very pretty story," she said. "He was an outlaw in Fresno when Horatio was working for Wells Fargo. Did some sea time himself, though Horatio said he never advanced beyond first mate. He had some grudge against the sea, so much so that he became a gambler on the riverboats for a time."

"A boa constrictor." Adele couldn't help but grimace.

"He was not unlike Mr. Sipes," the woman agreed. "Though he was as polished as any gentleman."

"Probably learned it on the steamboats," Rowena remarked.

"He made a friend of Horatio," said Lady Augusta. "Not with poverty-laden tales, of course. Just honesty and cleanliness, or so it seemed."

Adele didn't doubt her words, knowing the sheriff's largess and his almost boyish desire to believe in people.

"Horatio defended him like the devil when Wells Fargo demanded his arrest. Mr. Merriment too pushed him into a corner, a similar corner like yours."

"I don't follow." Adele leaned against the counter.

"The most unpleasant charlatans use instinct as their power," said the woman. "The man knew Horatio had been at sea and used it as a weapon."

"How?"

"Oh, the brotherhood of sailors or some such nonsense," Lady Augusta said with a sigh. "He tried to get Horatio to believe what Wells told him was a lie. But it was all there in black and white."

Nin looked at the elderly woman, her fingers on the cash register." What did the sheriff do?"

"The right thing, of course." She chuckled. "Horatio had a weapon much sharper than Mr. Merrimont's. Integrity."

"I had no integrity on my side," Adele said with a wan smile.

"Only sentiment."

Lady Augusta placed the wrapped packages on her knees and tapped at the ground with her cane, an indication she was ready to leave. She looked at Adele's limp figure. "Don't you think you'd better go out and retrieve your customers?"

Adele stared at her. "My what?"

"The ladies."

"I don't think they would come in again," said Adele.

"You told me when you first arrived here that you meant to have a presence," said Lady Augusta in a stern tone. "You don't cultivate a presence by cowering like a frightened rabbit inside your shop, do you?"

"They'll be the ones cowering like rabbits if I invite them in," Adele insisted. "They'll be too frightened to enter."

"Then you just *unfrighten* them," Lady Augusta declared, taking firm hold of the wheels of her chair. "You're a modern woman, and modern women aren't afraid of a damn thing."

Her words filled Adele with courage. She grabbed Nin's arm. "We'll get those geese back in here if we have to drag them in!"

Adele knew the moment they stepped onto the dusty road, they would need to find the right target. Mrs. Faderman was her obvious choice, but the woman was nowhere to be seen. She spotted Mrs. Lynn and her cousin emerging from the frosted glass doors of Dora's Tea Shop, the latter fussing with a lace handkerchief in her handbag. Adele pulled Nin across the street.

"Had a pleasant lunch, Mrs. Lynn?"

"What? Oh, yes, fine, fine." The woman's teetering walk made her reel back a little.

"Finest cucumber and parsley sandwiches I ever ate," Mrs. Nitt declared. "Can't get that in Red Gulch."

"I'm sorry we were distracted earlier," Adele said, taking Mrs. Nitt's arm. "I promise I'll devote my time just to you."

Mrs. Lynn's hands twitched. "That awful man —"

"You needn't worry," Nin assured her. "We chased him away."

Though it was clear the woman was still alarmed, Mrs. Nitt was only too willing to let herself be led back to the shop. As they crossed the street, the woman leaned into Adele's shoulder and whispered, "Did that wild beast attack you?"

"No, but he roamed all around my shop," Adele said. Several of the younger generation of prominent citizens were gathered not far from the doorway of Nin's shop. Among them was Vanessa Faderman, Mrs. Faderman's daughter. Adele spoke loudly, knowing Vanessa's rather sedate countenance hid a love of adventure.

The woman let out a gasp and dropped her handkerchief on the sidewalk. "Whatever did you do, Miss Gossling?"

"She went after him with a paper knife," Nin said.

Within fifteen minutes, Adele's shop was filled again.

~~~~~

In the late afternoon, Adele watched Mrs. Faderman and some of her followers lay a table in the middle of Bridge Street. Her usual select group expanded to a small sea of strange faces intrigued by the bone china and tiered platters. "Don't tell me she's holding one of her moveable tea parties," Adele snorted. "Today of all days?"

"Especially today of all days." Nin leaned against the display window. "She makes a show of it every year about this time. English tea time, she says."

Just then, Mrs. Faderman spotted them. "Ah, Miss Gossling!" She advanced with a congenial smile altogether too painted on her face. "Join us, won't you?"

"That can't be good," Nin mumbled.

Adele took her friend's hand. "Miss Branch and I would be delighted."

Though Nin had attended the tea parties before, it was clear the gray-haired woman had not meant to extend the invitation on that particular day. Her face soured like a dried grape hanging on a vine. "I don't think we have enough, unfortunately."

"I can drink my tea from a jar," Nin said with a sweet smile. "Would you like me to bring one?"

"That won't be necessary," said the woman in a brisk tone. She instructed the maid to hand out teacups and plates of frosted carrot cake and dainty cream cheese and olive sandwiches.

Nin made a sweeping gesture. "To community spirit, eh, Mrs. Faderman?"

The woman glared with swollen eyes. She turned to Adele. "Miss Gossling, we were hoping you could help us." Her head indicated the row of ladies who stood behind her.

"Help the *community*," Mrs. Abberton corrected.

"You know I'm always happy to do anything I can," Adele said, feeling both curious and amused. "For the community."

The woman beamed. "Since you have so much influence with the police —"

"You practically have a deputy badge yourself!" Mrs. Cricket declared.

The silver-haired woman gave her a silencing look. "We thought you could use your influence with your brother and the sheriff about —" her hand flitted behind her without turning around, "*them.*"

"Them?" Nin asked.

Mrs. Faderman was clearly losing her patience. "Those young men who have been parading around all morning in their vulgar attire."

"Don't tell us you're suddenly afraid to go to the sheriff yourself." Nin eyed her. "You've done it often enough."

"I was speaking to Miss Gossling," the woman snapped. "If you insist on clinging to her sash everywhere she goes, you should at least not interfere."

"I thought you were planning on speaking to him yourself," Adele said.

The woman's pince-nez dug into her cheek. "Well, I did, as a matter of fact."

"We all did," Mrs. Abberton said, her hand touching the tight curls at the nape of her neck. "After that dreadful man showed up."

"Then you don't need me, do you?" Adele asked.

"Sheriff Hatfield was very pleasant and courteous —" Mrs. Faderman began.

"But he wouldn't budge an inch." Mrs. Cricket sniffed as she fished out the largest piece of honey cake on the plate. "A most uncompromising man."

"I imagine not, after he heard about Mr. Sipes and his cat," Adele said dryly.

"He knows his assistant deputies will do their job," Nin added, "no matter how gaudy they look."

"This isn't about their tacky dress, Miss Gossling." The woman stiffened. "It's something far more serious."

"They're a pack of bumbling idiots!" Mrs. Abberton pushed at Mrs. Faderman's elbow. "*Tell* her, Irene."

Adele watched as the silver-haired woman rubbed specks of red dust that had swept the table from her fingers. "I'm afraid Hester is right. The situation is urgent."

"Situation?" Nin asked.

"Mr. Edison and his friends made an error in judgment earlier today," the woman said.

"If you mean because they didn't arrest Mr. Sipes, I would hardly expect them to storm my shop with a tiger roaming around in it," Adele said.

"I wasn't referring to that," said Mrs. Faderman. "I must admit, from what Vanessa told me, it sounded as if you had that situation well in hand."

"Be careful, or Adele might take that as a compliment," Nin sneered.

"I'm referring to the incident in Raleigh's," the woman continued. "They tried to arrest a relative of his in the store."

Adele's hand shook as she tried to balance the teacup.

"His uncle came down from Santa Barbara especially for the picnic, and Mr. Raleigh was showing him some of his wares," Mrs. Faderman said. "The man took a fancy to one of those ready-made hats for his daughter."

Adele couldn't help think of the many middle-aged men she had heard her father speak of who bought ready-made hats and anything else that smacked of youth for their "daughters."

"Well, naturally, Mr. Raleigh wouldn't charge him a penny, his being a relative and all."

"Naturally." Adele could only imagine one of Arrojo's well-known penny pinchers grinding his teeth behind a smiling insistence that anyone lay their hands on anything without paying for it.

"When he tried to leave the store with the hat, Mr. Edison tried to arrest him!" Mrs. Cricket said.

Adele looked from one to the other.

"Mr. Edison and his friends blocked the doorway just as he was about to go," said the silver-haired woman. "They insisted on seeing a sales slip. Of course, the man had none. Well, you can imagine what happened next."

"Yes," said Adele, feeling her cheeks flare as she pictured Edison with his striped suit. "I can imagine."

"He even had handcuffs!" Mrs. Lynn said with a shudder.

Adele set down her teacup. "Are you sure?"

Mrs. Faderman was immediately at her pince-nez. "Is there something the matter, Miss Gossling?"

"I only mean Sheriff Hatfield once told me he had a terrible experience involving subordinates with handcuffs," Adele said. "I know for a fact he doesn't allow anyone but Jackson and himself to use them."

"Imagine knowing a thing like that!" Mrs. Lynn exhaled.

"Not a thing for a young lady to know," Mrs. Abberton remarked.

"She's the deputy's sister. Of course she would know!" Nin

insisted.

"The sheriff would never allow mere assistant deputies to use handcuffs without his supervision," Adele continued. "He believes only well-trained men ought to handle them."

"Well, apparently, he changed his mind," Mrs. Faderman said, "or someone persuaded him to change it." She had dropped the pince-nez but was still looking at Adele with her keen eyes.

The weight of the woman's words sat on her shoulders like boulders. Had Hatfield really violated his own rules and given the sacred handcuffs to Edison?

"If he did, he had good reason, didn't he, Mrs. Faderman?" Nin was eyeing the woman with equal strength.

"Since our own requests have gone unnoticed," the woman said, her voice strained, "we thought you could use your influence to benefit the community."

Adele remained silent. Maybe she hadn't used the influence Mrs. Faderman claimed she had with the sheriff in a good way this time, if it was indeed true Edison had gone too far. Or maybe Hatfield was so convinced the thief was heading for Arrojo, he felt it was worth the risk of putting the handcuffs in Edison's bumbling hands and relied on the young man's sense of duty to guide him to do the proper thing with them.

"I don't believe I exaggerate when I say you owe it to the community to intervene," Mrs. Faderman said.

"She doesn't owe you a blessed thing!" Nin growled.

"You keep your tongue civil, Miss Branch." Mrs. Abberton snapped her hand out toward her as if she were going to slap her face.

All good sense dissipated into a wave of dust that brushed against Adele's face. She knew she couldn't reason away her guilt.

"You look a little ashen, dear." Mrs. Lynn peered at her.

"You ought to have more tea," Mrs. Nitt insisted, grabbing the pot from a maid's hands.

Adele looked at Mrs. Faderman. "If the sheriff felt it necessary to send Edison and the others, I trust his judgment, and I should hope you do too."

"You mean you won't go?" Mrs. Abberton dropped her fork. It landed in the red dust, and a maid swooped down to retrieve it, laying it carefully on the table.

"If you mean, will I tell the sheriff what he should or shouldn't do with his own deputies," Adele felt her throat tighten. "I certainly will not."

"You're quite willing to tell the sheriff what he should and shouldn't do when it comes to crime," the woman said with a sneer.

Adele bit her lip. "I've never told the sheriff how to do his work like some people I might mention."

Mrs. Lynn cleared her throat. "I'm sure Miss Gossling has a very good reason for refusing to do what we ask, Irene." Her voice was almost pleading.

"A sensible girl," Mrs. Nitt agreed. "Struck me as sensible from the first."

"Sensible!" Mrs. Abberton said. "Sheer stubbornness, that's what it is." She turned to Mrs. Faderman. "Irene, speak to her."

Adele almost wished she would. She felt more nervous by her silence than the ladies' insults and reprimands. Her breath slowed, and she leaned against the table to steady herself.

Mrs. Faderman's tone was surprisingly subdued. "Perhaps you'd care to explain, Miss Gossling."

"She just did," Nin said.

"I'm sure you could turn me into a toad if you chose, Miss Branch," the woman remarked, "like all mesmerizers."

Nin's face became inflamed with rage, the likes of which Adele had never seen. She looked like a devil woman. Adele put her arm around her friend's shoulders and whispered, "Go see to the shop, will you, dear?"

When Nin had stalked off, Adele said calmly, "Vicious insults won't do any good, Mrs. Faderman."

"It would be such a little thing to talk to the sheriff," Mrs. Lynn said in a soft voice.

She looked at the woman, so small and dirtied with the red dust that the wind seemed to rub all over her, the small face generous with wrinkles of a burdensome fright.

She eyed the ladies. "Don't any of you trust the sheriff anymore?"

Mrs. Faderman's voice echoed down the street, "We did until you came along."

"You don't mean that, Irene," Mrs. Lynn murmured.

Adele met the woman's unkind eyes. "What are you implying, Mrs. Faderman?" Her knees were trembling.

"The sheriff obviously holds you in high regard," said the woman. "Perhaps a little too high."

Adele stiffened. "Is that all?"

"Perhaps," Mrs. Faderman ventured, "you use that to your advantage more than you should."

"That's for him to judge, not you." Adele turned to go back to her shop.

Mrs. Faderman took hold of her arm. "May I give you some friendly advice?"

"A spanking would be more appropriate, Irene," Mrs. Abberton grumbled.

"What is the advice, Mrs. Faderman?" Adele stood tall.

"An adventuress doesn't always end up on the right side of society," the woman said.

"I don't consider helping the police catch murderers an adventure!"

"Oh, dear!" Mrs. Nitt brought her handkerchief to her lips.

"A young woman was murdered a few years ago, and her body was found at my house," Adele explained to the newcomer. "She was my neighbor and friend. I helped the police catch her killer."

"And you've been helping them ever since," Mrs. Faderman declared.

"Miss Gossling is very helpful," Mrs. Lynn said in a hurried voice.

"It's most disturbing," snapped Mrs. Abberton.

"I realize you all would prefer I answer the calling of marriage, children, and church," Adele continued, her voice ragged. "We were speaking earlier of possibilities. I see my possibilities as endless and my potential differently."

"That difference is very serious, Miss Gossling," Mrs. Faderman said. "I don't think you realize the damage you may cause to yourself and others."

A whirl of anger stirred in Adele. "I'm not a child, ma'am. I realize the consequences of my actions as well as anyone."

"Maybe you do." Her voice was sly. "But does the sheriff? More to the point, does he care?"

Adele stared. "What do you mean?"

"I mean, he may not be in his prime, but he has the eye for a pretty youthful figure," Mrs. Faderman declared.

The fury finally broke through Adele's composure. "Sheriff Hatfield is as decent a man as they come!"

"A proud man, certainly," she said in a dry voice. "Let me remind you of the words of the Good Book: 'Pride goeth before destruction.'" The woman regarded her with a righteous smile.

Adele felt as if her bones had turned into glass. In her most ladylike voice, she said, "Perhaps it's *you* who ought to heed those words, Mrs. Faderman."

"And just what do you mean by that, Miss Gossling?" The woman bent forward.

"I mean maybe your pride has gotten the better of you once too often."

"Irene only does what's good for the community," Mrs. Abberton insisted as she held out her plate for a lemon roll.

"Who appointed her judge and jury of what's good for this community?" Adele demanded.

With exaggerated dignity, Mrs. Faderman slid one of the

lemon rolls on a clean plate and covered it with a napkin. "Miss Branch has always liked my lemon rolls. I'm sure she's calmed down enough for you to give it to her."

Adele glared at her, then turned to ladies. "I gather none of you were at the town council meeting yesterday."

Shaking heads went all around.

"And I'm sure Mrs. Faderman neglected to tell you about the very *serious* discussion that went on during that meeting," she continued.

Eyes turned toward the silver-haired woman still holding the plate with both her hands.

"There was nothing important at the meeting." Her face remained immobile, though her eyes were melted, as if she knew she was trapped.

"On the contrary," said Adele, feeling her breath gaining power. "I think it was most important."

"That you should know about it —"

"The affairs of the council aren't a secret, are they, Mrs. Faderman?"

The woman remained silent.

"A serious discussion?" Mrs. Cricket was now looking at the woman. "You told us there was nothing new, Irene."

"I didn't want to alarm you, Belinda," she said with a tight laugh.

"But according to Miss Gossling, there is something we should know about?" Mrs. Abberton raised her eyebrow.

"Well." The woman put down the plate. "Well, the sheriff did mention an unfortunate incident involving some of the business districts in the county. Far away from us, of course."

"Surely, we can be more accurate, can't we?" Adele asked. "A thief has been making his way through the county."

"Oh!" Mrs. Lynn covered her mouth with both hands.

"But Mrs. Faderman decided —"

"The council decided!"

"The council decided — with Mrs. Faderman's persuasion and encouragement — that it would be best not to warn us about it."

"But —" Mrs. Lynn ventured.

"That's why the sheriff sent the deputies out this morning," Adele continued. "Since Bridge Street business owners weren't to be told their shops might be robbed at any moment, he thought it best to have Edison and the rest keep a watchful eye on our merchandise. And he did it without telling you because he knew Mrs. Faderman wouldn't approve!"

Mrs. Faderman's whole being turned to granite, from the pallor of her face down to her rigid posture. "This is unworthy of you, Miss Gossling."

Adele looked at her for a moment. All the courage in her left and she said in a soft voice, "You have done your duty, ma'am. Now I've done mine."

She slowly made her way back to her shop, leaving behind a bewildered silence. Her eyes fell on a child's wagon squeezed between the writing paper display and parchment rolls. Frayed and almost colorless, the two large wheels showed the splinters of many years' hard labor as the bed rested on the ground with a few odds and ends.

"Zephyr!"

The blond head of Zephyr Brown, the town's junk collector, popped up from behind the counter. Her hair was more unkept than dirty, as one might expect from someone in her position. The waves, in fact, were as wild as those on Nin, her nemesis. Zephyr's blond hair had not a strand of gray even though she was well into her fifties.

"Where's Nin?"

"Hightailed it the minute I come in." Zephyr's voice was unusually squeaky and light for someone so slow-moving. "Ain't no use leaving the place to someone who's going to antagonize the customers, you know."

Nin appeared from the back of the shop, her voice sharp.

"You're no customer. You're the devil's wife!"

Zephyr hitched her coat around her and gave a good-natured grin. "Only been a wife once, and he was no devil. Rather be a witch than somebody's wife now, devil or not."

"I'm no witch!" came the screeching response.

"Didn't figure on naming names," the woman answered, "but if we're getting into particulars —"

"Get out!" Nin said.

Zephyr chewed on her lower lip. "I'll just take that twine you promised me, Adele, and be on my way."

Adele gave her a wan smile. She reached into one of the closed cabinets for the twine she always saved for the woman, coiling it into a bow. Her jerking hands betrayed the anger still boiling inside her.

Zephyr squinted at her. "Honey, you look like somebody just stomped on the last of your pride."

Mrs. Faderman's words echoed back to Adele: *Pride goeth before destruction.* "Not mine," she murmured. "Someone else's."

"The sheriff's?"

Adele stared. "How did you know?"

"Know everything, see everything." The woman opened her eyes wide, and the blue in them sparkled like diamonds. "Maybe more than that cat with her conjuring, eh?"

Nin sprang forward, grabbing the edge of her coat. Adele soothed her, sending her to the other side of the shop to arrange the gift cards on the table.

"You know how she feels about that," she said in a chilly voice.

"Wild cat, that one," said Zephyr with a shrug. "She's going to scratch somebody's eyes out someday." She turned her eyes on Adele. "She'd scratch Mrs. Faderman's eyes out in a red-hot second if you'd give the word."

Still seething from the attack, she said, "I can do my own scratching very well."

Zephyr propped her elbow up on the glass counter, leaning

her cheek in her hand. "Suppose you tell me what you were sparring about out there."

Adele found herself telling Zephyr everything as a child might confess a pardonable sin to her mother. She finished with, "She thinks I'm going to hurt someone someday by helping the police."

"The old hag!" Nin, who had been lingering nearby, wandered back.

"But not far off the mark," Zephyr said with half-closed eyes. "That's why you're hopping mad."

"Maybe it is," Adele admitted. "I was the one who convinced Sheriff Hatfield to send those boys out."

"Well, you made a whale of a mistake," the junk collector said with a chuckle. "I saw them sashaying around like they were politicians or something. Don't expect that's what the sheriff wanted."

"Jack tried to warn me about Edison," Adele said.

"You tell her all this? Mrs. Faderman, I mean."

She shook her head. "The sheriff didn't think she would look too kindly upon me if she knew."

"Who wants her kindness?" Nin said. "Best not to have it anyway."

"She don't think too kindly of you as it is," Zephyr pointed out. "But you're not on her bad side yet. Might do a lot of damage if you were."

"I care more about obeying the sheriff's orders," Adele said. "And he's following her lead on this."

"Can't see you obeying or disobeying any man," Zephyr said with a smile.

"Certainly not one who's sweet on you," Nin added. This made Zephyr burst out laughing as Adele felt her face turn scarlet.

"Now they know part of it, at least," she said with a sigh.

"What's done is done," Nin agreed.

"Well, then suppose I help you clean up this place?" Zephyr

pinched her cheek in a friendly way. "Might cheer you up some."

They picked up the spilled cards, unrolled paper, and other things out of place.

"Oughtn't to put expensive stuff out in plain sight like that," Zephyr remarked, staring down at the pens. "Say, where's that ugly-looking one with all them snakes on it?"

"The Montache pen?"

"Don't tell me someone actually *bought* it!" The woman gave a clownish smile as she stood with her hands on her hips. "Well, maybe I don't blame them, what with gold prices."

Adele dropped to her knees and looked at all the displays. The Montache box was empty. "Nin, you didn't sell it while I was away and forgot to tell me, did you?"

"I wouldn't even give it away," the dark-haired woman declared.

"Then it's gone!" Adele's voice came out in a shriek.

"Now, now," Zephyr patted her arm, "likely just somewhere around here that we ain't got to."

All three searched every inch of floor and shelf space. Zephyr wasn't shy about getting on her hands and knees and bending down. The pen was nowhere to be found.

Nin narrowed her eyes. "Adele, look in her wagon. Look in her filthy pockets!"

"Now you just hold on a minute, you cat!" The woman pointed a finger at her. "I may not be top drawer, but I ain't no thief."

Adele's knees felt weak. "Who came in while I was gone?"

"No one," said Nin. "They were all at the tea party."

"Nobody here when I come in," Zephyr said. "The door was closed like it'd been closed for some time." She eyed Nin, who glared back at her.

"Did the bell ring at all? Could you see anyone inside before you went in?"

"I tell you no one came in except her!"

"Someone might have while we were gone." Adele felt even more ill.

"I don't think so," Nin said.

Adele pressed her hand.

"That still don't mean it didn't catch someone's eye from the window," said Zephyr.

"Maybe it caught yours!" Nin glared. "Ask her why she isn't more surprised it's missing."

Adele watched as Zephyr placed the twine in her wagon. The woman was rolling it into a ball like yarn, but her hands were exacting.

"She might be involved with a den of thieves," Nin insisted. "I wouldn't put it past a she-demon like her."

"I don't know nothing about no thieves," Zephyr replied.

"That's not what I heard." Nin crossed her arms over her chest.

"Hear lots of things in a town like this," the woman replied calmly. "I heard things about you that weren't so complimentary, but you don't see me throwing around accusations."

"You're not surprised the pen is gone, are you?" Adele asked quietly.

The woman lay the ball down. "Honey, I been around too long to be much surprised about anything."

Adele collapsed on the floor, oblivious to the red dust scattering all over her skirt. "Mrs. Faderman was right."

"Mrs. Faderman is never right about anything," her friend insisted.

"It ain't your fault," said Zephyr quietly, "but the sheriff's reputation might be on the line."

Adele stared at her. "What do you mean?"

"He sent his deputies to make sure nothing was stolen from the shops, right?" the woman pointed out. "Well, if something's been taken, the council might blame him for incompetence or whatever fancy word they find."

Adele rose, dusting off her skirt. "Then we'll have to warn him."

"You don't have to tell him it was me who found out, do you?" Zephyr gave her an itchy look.

"Why would that matter?"

"Because he'd come to the same conclusion I have!" Nin growled.

"I just would rather keep the police at a safe distance," said the woman. "I ain't got a sheriff sweet on me like you." She chuckled and pulled her wagon out of the shop.

~~~~~

Jackson and Sheriff Hatfield were standing outside the Arrojo Police Station with a bearded, wiry man. Adele recognized Mr. Ellingsworth, the owner of the antique shop in town. She was almost relieved to see Edison sitting at his desk and the other young men, still in their gaudy suits, slouched in chairs around him.

Mr. Ellingsworth glanced at the two women through owl spectacles, mumbling something to the sheriff, and bid them good day as he slunk down the street.

"What did he want?" Adele watched the man disappear into Raleigh's store.

"Police business." Jackson kissed her cheek. "Nothing that need concern you."

"It seems the consensus is that nothing at all should concern a young lady like me," she said warily. "Mrs. Faderman and I had quite a discussion about it."

"Spiteful harpy!" Nin snarled.

Adele's hands felt sticky inside her gloves. She could not look at Hatfield, though he was looking at her.

"I'm glad to see them back." She nodded toward the assistant deputies.

The sheriff's look intensified as he remained silent. Her brother seemed not to notice. "Mr. Ellingsworth's shop was hit by our mysterious thief. Some antique medals were stolen, quite valuable, he insists."

The news hit her like a blow to her head. "It wouldn't have mattered if they hadn't been out, then. No, it wouldn't have mattered."

Hatfield glanced at Jackson. "I think your sister needs a glass of water."

She felt Jackson's powerful arms around her shoulders as he led her to the leather chair Hatfield used, worn into comfort. A glass was put in front of her, and as she drank, she could almost feel the gritty dust penetrating the walls of the station.

"You all right now, Del?" he asked in a gentle voice.

She could not find her voice, so Nin spoke for her. "Her most valuable pen was stolen."

Hatfield's gathered features made his usually pleasant countenance like an angry bull. She felt a wave of fear, knowing the hidden rage in this mild-mannered man could come out at the most unexpected provocations.

"*Edison!*"

The young man jumped out of his chair. The others leaned forward and grabbed the edge of theirs as if to steady themselves for the blow they fully expected to come in due time.

"Sheriff?" the young man's voice broke.

"Miss Gossling has just informed me a valuable pen was stolen from her store."

"Sir!"

"That makes *two*, Edison. Two." Hatfield shook his fingers in the man's face. "First you bumble things with Mr. Raleigh's cousin —"

"Uncle," Nin said in a timid voice.

" — then you let the thief steal from two shops and heaven knows how many more."

"Well, but, sir —"

The roar Adele was expecting came with a vengeance. "Do

you mind telling me just what the devil you and the lads were doing all day?"

"We were patrolling, just like you told us to."

"Flirting, more like it," Jackson murmured.

"No, sir, truly!" The young man tossed his head back to the others in the room as if looking for confirmation. They all gave violent shakes of their heads and turned away from the door with a wince.

"All the young ladies were in town in their Sunday best," Jackson pointed out.

"We did everything you told us, Sheriff."

"Do you realize," the sheriff said slowly, "that I've had to defend your gallivanting around in your clown suits and staring fish-eyed at every person who passed you by all morning? I've had to make apologies and promises to Mr. Raleigh and his family because you seem to think you're playing a part in a moving picture!"

"I warned you about giving him the handcuffs," her brother mumbled.

"I can no longer justify sending you out in the first place!"

"I assure you, sir, we were looking about us every moment." Edison cowered in his chair.

"But you weren't actually *seeing* what you were looking at!" Hatfield thundered. "Is this how I taught you to do your job?" His face drew beads of perspiration in his anger.

Adele touched the sheriff's arm. "I know they did their best to keep any crime from being committed, Sheriff."

"The lads I can understand," Hatfield went on. "They've no training other than yours. But you? With two uncles on the force, I expected better."

Adele could barely hold herself back from rushing to Edison's side, and even Nin looked sympathetic. Her brother was clearly beginning to feel sorry for the red-faced young man who was visibly shaken.

"Sheriff," Jackson ventured, "if the thief was successful in three other towns, he would be difficult to spot even for the most experienced officer."

Hatfield's tone was sharp but no longer thundering. "I'm prepared to give you another chance, my lad."

Edison's eyes were bright as lamps as he stood up like a soldier awaiting command.

"Take the young men and go straight away to the picnic. Interview every single person there about what they saw today. Every citizen and every visitor. I don't want to hear you've been wasting your time on food and chatter with the ladies."

Edison's head bobbed, and he turned to leave. The sheriff yanked him back.

"I didn't say I was finished, did I?"

The young man stood again in salute.

"Ask every business owner in Arrojo if anything is missing from his or her shop."

"They wouldn't tell us, sir," Edison mumbled.

"You damn well better make them, then!" he shouted. "Report your findings to me as soon as I get there. And don't even *think* about sending one of the lads to do it. Is that understood?"

The assistant deputy's head bobbed again.

"Well, go to it, man!" the sheriff snarled.

Edison scurried with his head bent so low that he looked almost half his size. The assistant deputies followed him, none of them daring to look at the sheriff.

The moment they left, Hatfield's usual good nature returned. "That ought to get a fire started in his belly, eh, Jackson?"

"You were very hard on him, Sheriff," Adele said quietly.

"They really did try," Nin chimed in.

"Edison knows I don't tolerate slackness," said Hatfield. "I may have been severe, but it will make a better lawman out of him, and that boy has a future."

"I can't imagine what makes you think so," Jackson said dryly.

"You haven't my experience, Deputy," said Hatfield in a surprisingly grated tone. "I've seen many bumbling fools enter the station house doors in San Francisco and emerge chief officers and detectives. They were as dedicated as Edison."

"Maybe that's your trouble, Jack," Adele said. "Maybe you don't have the same dedication."

He stiffened. "I'm here, aren't I?"

"And doing the sheriff no favors by it," Nin snapped. "You ought to be more grateful he hired you at all."

Jackson's face grew a little white. He wandered to his desk and retrieved a few sheets of scribbled paper. "We're recording every item stolen so we can track them down later."

Adele held out her hand. "I suppose I have a right to see it since I'm the latest victim?"

The handwriting was in the sheriff's large, slow letters as if he had taken precautions in writing them down:

Vargas:
Ladies' gold watch
Ladies' bracelet
Cigarette lighter
Blue Springs:
Belt buckle, gold, ruby inlay
Watch and chain
Rosa Gris:
3 gold-framed cameos
4 engagement rings
Brooch, Civil War widow

She handed the list back to Hatfield. "A pen, you said?" the sheriff asked, poised with a pencil.

"A Montache Special."

"That monstrosity with the snakes and gaudy stone?" Jackson could not keep the smirk from his face.

"That monstrosity, dear brother, is the latest fashion and worth quite a lot, as pens go," Adele retorted.

"More than Mr. Ellingsworth's whatever-it-is," Nin said.

Hatfield leaned back. "Any strange characters come into your shop today?"

"The dandy and the man in the wrinkled suit," said Nin.

Jackson regarded her with his easy smile. "You're as observant as any Anspach detective, Miss Branch."

"Considering the filthy nature of their work, Mr. Gossling," she answered with just as easy a smile, "I would rather be a hog farmer."

"It's a start," said Hatfield. "Mr. Ellingsworth couldn't tell us a thing. Or wouldn't."

"Two men were fighting over the pen," Adele said. "Mr. Lyman and another customer." She leaned over the sheriff's shoulder. "Did Mr. Ellingsworth say anything about the medal?"

"Congressional medal, late eighteenth century, I believe," said Jackson.

"A Revolutionary War medal?" Adele glanced at her friend.

"Is that important?"

"Possibly," she said. "The man in the wrinkled suit said he was a collector of such relics."

"That would hardly explain the other thefts," Jackson pointed out.

"I think it would be a good idea to question him anyway," said Hatfield. "He didn't give his name, I gather?"

"He was a stranger in town," she said. "I'm certain of that."

"Probably staying at the hotel, then."

"And Mr. Lyman?" Jackson asked. "If he took part in this argument, we can't be sure he isn't involved in something."

The sheriff leaned back. "The Sacramento police think this might be someone who comes into town, takes what he can, and moves on. That would hardly make any permanent citizen of ours a likely suspect."

"If you question Mr. Lyman, you'll be wasting your time," Nin remarked. "He couldn't take a stick of candy from a baby."

"Too prudent?" Adele agreed.

Her friend shook her head. "Too fainthearted."

Even the sheriff gave one of his hearty laughs at this.

"He may have accidentally taken it." Adele was thoughtful.

"What do you mean?" Jackson asked.

"He was the last one to have it in his hand. He was going to buy it, in fact, when Mr. Sipes and his cat came along and frightened everyone away."

"Ma told me about that. She said you handled yourself very well." Admiration seeped into his voice.

She laid her hand on the sheriff's strong forearm, though she removed it quickly when she saw the glance from her brother, whose modes of behavior were more aligned to what they had been taught in San Francisco society.

Jackson cleared his throat. "Why do you think Mr. Lyman might have taken the pen by accident, Del?"

"He and the others ran off when Mr. Sipes appeared."

"The craven." Jackson gritted his teeth.

"Craven or not, it's not inconceivable he may have left the shop with the pen in hand without realizing it.

"I've the eeriest feeling about Mr. Sipes." Nin shivered. "The Generous Ones are not looking favorably upon him."

"We received reports last night of this man roaming around town with a wild animal." Jackson turned to his superior. "I thought we told Edison to run him out of town if he saw him."

"Edison couldn't run a dead chicken out of town," Nin snarled.

Hatfield scowled in agreement. "I think we've had ample evidence of how reliable Edison is when it comes to holiday hullabaloo."

"I agree with Miss Branch," Jackson said. "A confident man, a stranger in town, no less, is apt to be suspicious."

"But he was in plain view the entire time he was with us," said Adele.

"Entire time?" Jackson looked up with alarm.

As Adele explained, she watched as his usually refined countenance gathered with rage. "Of all the insolent, dastardly —"

"Now, wait, Jack." Adele held up her hand.

"He said his cat liked women and would never hurt one," Nin chimed in.

"I don't like the sound of it either," said the sheriff, "but these charlatans do all they can to appeal to the ladies. I saw it often on the pier when I was a captain."

"I don't like that he was playing games with you, Del," Jackson growled.

"I thought that too at first," she said. "But I think the magnifying glass genuinely fascinated him."

"Fascinated or not, he had no right to bribe you into letting him examine it," Nin declared.

"Don't worry, we'll get him out of town," Hatfield assured them. "Is there anyone else you think we ought to speak to?" He took up his pencil again. "Anyone take an unusual interest in the pen other than Mr. Lyman and the man in the wrinkled suit?"

"That Brown woman," Nin said. "She was in the shop alone for a time. I told Adele to search her things, but she was too trusting." She eyed her friend.

"She visits my shop all the time," Adele insisted. "She had plenty of chances to steal from me before this. Why would she choose today?"

"Holidays are always chaotic with all the strangers in town," her brother said. "It's easy to shift blame on someone else."

"Zephyr and I are friends." She stiffened.

"Her friendly hands were certainly all over your wares." Nin sniffed.

"Sheriff, you just said the thief is most likely a stranger in these parts," Adele pointed out. "Zephyr is hardly a stranger in Arrojo."

"Nevertheless," Hatfield put aside the list, "she roams about the towns here quite a lot. It's conceivable she might know something."

"She's the one who discovered the pen was missing and didn't want us to tell you," Nin said. "Doesn't that make her suspicious right there?"

"Not necessarily," Hatfield answered. "People like her are rarely willing to talk to the police, even under the best of circumstances. Most lawmen are quick to suspect them because of their wayward nature. But wayward people are also usually the first to know things the police don't."

Adele rose from the chair, brushing her hands on her skirt. "Then you think we ought to see her just to find out if she knows anything that might help us?"

Jackson eyed her. "Sheriff, I think we ought to send Del and Miss Branch to the picnic and handle this matter on our own."

"My dear brother," she said, trying to keep her voice low, "had it not been for my error in judgment regarding Edison and the lads, there might not have been any crime. Doesn't that make Nin and I just as responsible to help catch the thief as you and the sheriff?"

Jackson drummed his fingers on the wooden desk. They made a hollow echo in the empty office. "Sir?" He glanced at the sheriff.

"I'd like Adele to be with us when we speak to Mrs. Brown," said Hatfield. "I don't think she'll say much without someone there she trusts. I have no objection to either of these ladies accompanying us to see Mr. Lyman and the other fellow."

They called on Mr. Lyman at Mrs. Taylor's boarding house first. They found him in the parlor, leafing through a business magazine while he waited for the other boarders to come down, as they were all going to the picnic together.

"Miss Gossling!" He jumped up when he saw Adele. "Just the person I wanted to see. I ask your forgiveness for my inexcusable behavior today."

"As well you should, sir," Jackson said.

Adele gave her brother a look. "I can hardly blame you, Mr. Lyman." She leaned on the end of her parasol. "Seeing a wild beast close at hand like that is enough to frighten anyone away."

He seemed uneasy. "Well, I don't know if I would call that impertinent man a wild beast. He didn't even look at the pen!"

"I was referring to Mr. Sipes and his cat," she said dryly.

"Oh," he said. "Oh, yes. Well, *I* was referring to my argument with that impossible man."

"What was inexcusable was your decrepitude, sir." Jackson gave him such a hard look that the young man almost withered in his seat. "You left my sister and the other ladies alone, possibly to be torn to shreds by a wild animal."

"Including an elderly woman in a movable chair," Hatfield said, equally harsh, "who has more audacity in her little finger than you have in your entire well-dressed figure."

The young man pressed his hands together. "I see what you mean now. My apologies to Lady Augusta, Sheriff. And to you again, Miss Gossling." He bowed his head. "I'm ready to purchase that pen at any price you ask." He removed his wallet from the inside pocket of his coat.

"That would be fine if the pen weren't missing, sir," Hatfield said.

"Missing?"

"I imagine you're going to tell us you know nothing about it." The sheriff eyed him.

"Of course I know nothing about it!" The young man's face turned scarlet. He lowered his voice, glancing toward the stairs. "I've held a prominent position at the bank for five years, Sheriff."

"Your position, as far as I remember, is that of a cashier," Jackson said with a sardonic smile.

"All the same, do you imagine I would still be there were I not a most trustworthy person?

77

Jackson said, "Your position, sir, may be an admirable one but certainly not requiring the kind of trust you imply."

The man stiffened. "I suppose it isn't too much to ask that we continue this conversation in my room? I don't want to alarm Mrs. Taylor."

"I shouldn't think so," Adele remarked, "after the woman had to endure Millie Gibb's dead body in one of her rooms earlier this year."

"She couldn't stand a dead person and a thief under her roof," Nin agreed.

"I am not a —" The man's voice lowered again. "If you'll come this way."

When they reached Mr. Lyman's room, he sat on the bed, grasping the edges of the blanket. "I have not now nor ever in my life stolen anything. I never even stole a penny from my dear mother's purse when I was a child."

"We understand there was quite a bit of chaos when this man Mr. Sipes and his cat appeared," said Hatfield.

Mr. Lyman shuddered. "The gall of the man!"

"My sister told us you were the last to handle the pen," said Jackson. "It would be understandable if, in the fear of the moment, you ran off with it in your hand."

"I told you, Deputy, I have the utmost moral standing." The young man sniffed. "I would never walk out of a shop with an item I never bought, not even in fright. And if I had, I would have brought it back immediately with my profuse apologies."

"That doesn't alter the fact you were last to be seen with it," Jackson argued. "What, then, did you do with it?"

The man grunted. "I threw it on the floor, I believe. Yes, I threw it down." He looked at Adele with appeasing eyes. "For the third time, I apologize for my unmanly behavior, Miss Gossling." He looked so miserable that Adele gave him a comforting smile.

"We would like to search your room, sir," said Hatfield. "A matter of procedure to eliminate you as a suspect."

"Certainly not!"

"Then you'll force us to come back with a warrant," the sheriff said in a quiet voice.

Jackson swung open the door. "Mrs. Taylor will have to hear about it, since it's her house. Shall I call her?"

The young man cowered as if a ghost had just appeared at the window. "Don't do that, please. You know how particular she is. You saw how she was when Miss Gibb —" He swallowed. "Search, if you must, but I would appreciate it if you would do so as quietly and quickly as possible. The others are getting ready for the picnic."

Adele knew her first instinct about Mr. Lyman had been right. He simply couldn't be the thief. His strained neck, flushed skin, and starched bow tie, indeed, his entire manner, pointed toward a man so aware of the impression he was making on others that the very idea of stealing would be abhorrent to him. Even a tiny risk of discovery would be enough to deter him.

She stepped outside in the hall with Nin.

"He's too fainthearted to even conceive of the pettiest crime," she said in a low voice.

"The pigeon-livered coward," her friend snorted.

As Adele expected, their search turned up nothing and with a quick apology, Hatfield sent the man on his way.

"He could have hidden it," Jackson pointed out as they left the boarding house. "In his office, maybe. He had time. And where better to hide stolen goods than a bank?"

"Your sense of honor is clouding your judgment, Jack," said his sister. "If a man can leave women to handle a wild animal on their own, he would hardly have the courage to steal a pen or the foresight to conceal it."

Hatfield nodded. "He probably threw it down on the floor in his haste to get away. That doesn't mean the actual thief couldn't have found it there."

"If he did, it would have been a most degenerative sort of

criminal." Her brother's eyes set. "Only such a man would take advantage of turmoil to steal."

"All criminals have their own brand of sickness, Jackson." the sheriff reminded him.

They headed for the Arrojo Hotel. People brushed past Adele, knocking their baskets against her shoulder. Amid apologies, their excited chatter and laughter eased her melancholy.

Jackson said in a low voice, "We don't want to arouse suspicion."

"I don't think people will find it suspicious that we're on the street," Hatfield observed. "They know about Mr. Sipes and his cat and probably think we're looking for him."

"Maybe we oughtn't to go to the picnic," Adele said with a sigh. "I don't feel much like celebrating."

"You can't let a stolen pen deflate your community spirit," the sheriff said.

Nin pressed her hand inside the crook of her arm. "We have to show Mrs. Faderman we have as much community spirit as she has, don't we?"

Adele smiled. "I suppose after three years, I've a right to that spirit as much as she has."

"Why, Adele!"

She felt a tightness in her chest as she turned around to meet Missy Grace's smile. They were good friends, but Missy was also the editor and owner of the *Arrojo Courier*, always ready to sniff out a story like a hog in a truffle patch.

"You look lovely, Missy." The young woman had traded in her usual starched suit for a summer dress and a hat with a long sash that fell down her back.

"You're going in the wrong direction if you're heading to the picnic," she said.

"I've some business to take care of first." Adele tried to return the smile. She was thankful Hatfield and Jackson had wandered on down the street.

"Oh?" Missy's intelligent face became alert. "Police business?"

"Don't be such a busybody," Nin snapped.

"I wasn't trying to be, Miss Branch." Missy was always cheerful in the face of Nin's indelicate manner.

"Will you do me a great favor?" Adele fished into her purse and pulled out a handful of bills. "Mrs. Wrigley and her pupils will be at the picnic, and I promised them gum drops and candy sticks, but I won't get to Hyde's in time."

Missy lingered a little after Adele handed her the money. "There's nothing else you want to tell me?"

"Nothing that concerns you," Nin said.

Adele pressed her hand. "Nothing." Her voice lowered. "Yet."

The two women exchanged a meaningful look as Missy retreated, stepping into the confectionary with a wave of her hand.

Both women breathed a sigh of relief. "You shouldn't have hinted you might have a story for her," Nin grumbled.

"People here disapprove of her work on the paper as much as they disapprove of my work with the police," Adele remarked. "We're allies as well as friends."

"Maybe you are," Nin said. "I'm an ally to no one but you."

Adele smiled at the bald loyalty and threaded her hand through her friend's.

The men were already engaged in conversation with the hotel proprietors, Mr. And Mrs. Bell, when they reached the hotel. A guest named Mr. Fields fit the description Adele gave of the man in the wrinkled suit.

Mr. Fields answered their knock right away. He was holding a hanger with trousers and a jacket in one hand and held a shoe-horn in the other. "Yes? I'm in a hurry."

The sheriff glanced at Jackson. "We may need to delay you, sir."

"What the devil — oh, how do you do?" He saw Adele and Nin and bowed. "Really, this is most inconvenient."

"I'm afraid it can't be helped." Hatfield held up his badge as he gently pushed open the door.

"As a matter of fact, Sheriff," Mr. Fields said, "I just received an urgent telegram, and I really must catch the two o'clock train." He suddenly seemed aware of the mess in the room and threw an embarrassed glance toward the ladies.

"Which train, if I may ask?" said Jackson.

"You may not, Deputy." The man's eyes narrowed. "As an American citizen, I assume I still retain some rights to privacy."

"True, sir," said Jackson. "But there's a crime involved. Theft, to be exact."

"A what?"

"I think you heard him." Hatfield suddenly looked imposing as his tall figure filled the smallness of the room.

"Yes, well, I'd like to help you, but, as I said, I'm in a hurry." Mr. Fields threw some linen into a trunk sitting on the bed and slammed it shut. Adele realized he was flustered not by the possibility that the police thought him to be involved in a crime but by the intrusion of women into his orderly masculine space.

In a soft voice, she said to Jackson, "Mr. Fields might be more comfortable if Nin and I waited in the hall."

"Thank you, miss," Mr. Fields said with a bow.

She pulled her friend out of the room. They couldn't see much, as the door was open only a sliver, but they could hear everything quite well.

"Mr. Fields," said the sheriff. "You were in Miss Gossling's establishment today, correct?"

"I was, sir."

"We're told you had quite a row with Mr. Lyman over a fountain pen."

"Who? Oh, that fop," Mr. Fields said. "One of those modern young men who cares more about his appearance than his values."

"That same pen was stolen from my sister's store," said Jackson.

There was a pause. "Are you sure?"

"My sister doesn't tell tales." His booming voice echoed in the hallway.

"Really, Adele," Nin whispered. "He acts as if you can't defend yourself."

"I wasn't implying she was lying, sir," Mr. Fields said, "only that she might be mistaken. There was a little, well, mayhem in the place. I'm sure she told you about it."

"The gold cat, you mean." Hatfield nodded.

"And you say now that pen is missing? Well, well, so the little fop is a thief!" There was a hint of satisfaction in Mr. Fields' voice.

"We believe Mr. Lyman had nothing to do with it," said Jackson.

"But you think I did?" The man's voice was ragged with agitation. "Why? Because I'm a stranger in town?"

"We're checking on travelers and suspicious people as a matter of routine," Hatfield said in his usual firm but patient way.

"If it's suspicious people you're looking for, I might be able to help you."

There was a pause where Adele could imagine Hatfield and her brother exchanging a look.

"When I was coming here from the telegraph office, I saw a woman enter your sister's store," he said. "A most suspicious-looking person, I can assure you."

"Can you describe this woman?" Jackson asked.

"She was sort of scruffy with sallow skin and yellow hair," he said. "She was most peculiar, dragging a child's wagon behind her."

"Zephyr," Adele murmured.

"When was this?" Hatfield asked.

"I don't wear a watch, Sheriff." The man gave a loud sniff. "It wasn't long after lunch, though, as I received word of the telegram when I was having my meal at the hotel. So you see, gentlemen," the bed springs gave another creak, "I'm no thief. Certainly, I would never soil my hands with such a hideous object as that pen. If you would have seen it —"

"I have seen it," said Jackson. "It might not be a beauty, sir, but it was valuable. So was the Congressional medal stolen from the antique shop here in town."

"I beg your pardon?"

"A Revolutionary War medal," Jackson said. "I was told you collect such things."

"So I do," he said.

"My sister said she recommended you visit Mr. Ellingsworth's shop," Jackson continued. "He's the owner of the antique store. Did you?"

"I might have." The hard sound of the trunk dropping to the floor made both women jump. "I'm afraid I haven't time to indulge your fantastic notions any further. I told you what I saw."

"Perhaps you have time to tell us what this urgent business of yours is?" asked Hatfield.

There was silence before the man answered, "It's of a very personal nature."

"This is an investigation, Mr. Fields." The sheriff's voice was final. Adele had come to admire the way Hatfield always knew how to make his point without being frightening or alienating.

"You insist you're above suspicion, but you refuse to tell us why you must leave town right away," Jackson said.

Hatfield's voice was softer as he said, "We will be, of course, discreet as much as we can."

Adele heard the deep creak of the bedsprings again. "I'm engaged to be married."

"Congratulations," said the sheriff.

"My fiancée's father, well, he's not keen on his daughter marrying a man considerably older than herself."

"I see." Hatfield's voice grew softer, though it sounded to Adele like the words were dropping on the floor like heavy weights.

"He had some young whippersnapper in mind for her, the son of one of his business associates. But, well, we're in love." This last came out in a bashful tone.

"Go on," said Jackson.

"I just received a cable from my fiancé that her father has taken her to Monterey for the holiday. It was a very sudden decision, and she believes he's asked this young whippersnapper there as well."

"I understand," Hatfield said. "If you will allow us to search your things, as a matter of routine, we'll phone the station and ask them to hold the train for you."

"Thank you, Sheriff. That's very decent of you." Mr. Fields sounded calm for the first time.

Both men emerged from the room a few minutes later, their search having come up empty. They made their way to the front room and Hatfield asked, "Miss Branch, can you verify Mr. Field's story that Zephyr Brown arrived at the stationery store after lunch?"

"Then you know it was her he was describing," Adele said.

"It wasn't too difficult to see that," Jackson said with a grimace.

"I don't keep track of time, Sheriff," Nin said. "I can't verify anything."

"Where were you when Mrs. Brown came in?"

Adele saw her friend growing shifty, and she took her arm in a reassuring way.

"I suppose I was in the back," she said. "I came to the front when I heard Adele's voice."

"Where were you?" Jackson turned to his sister.

She gave him a wary look. "Arguing with Mrs. Faderman on the street."

The sheriff chuckled. "Thank you, ladies." He gave them a quick bow. "That's very helpful to us."

Nin gave him a crooked smile and turned away.

"It's conceivable, then, that Mrs. Brown could have been in the shop for some time before Del came back," Jackson said.

"Enough time to put a pen and anything else that caught her fancy in that grimy wagon of hers," Nin remarked.

"Zephyr would never do such a thing," Adele insisted.

She looked at the sheriff for confirmation as he held the door open for them, but his expression showed more doubt than it had at the station earlier.

Zephyr was closing her junk shop. It was little more than shaky wooden panels nailed together with a straw roof. Adele couldn't help but feel saddened for the woman whose intelligence and insight had been welcoming to her compared to the stoic narrow-mindedness of some of Arrojo's citizens. But Zephyr was almost cheerful about her rather dismal surroundings at the crossroad between Quarry Lane and the train station blocking the more prominent side of town.

The woman grinned and waved, opening her door again with a creak. "I don't got much in the way of tea, but you're welcome to it, Sheriff," she said. "Got some of them fine food left over from the street party this afternoon." She winked at Adele. "The maids always smuggle me some before Mrs. Faderman throws it away."

"This is not a social call, Mrs. Brown," said Jackson.

She eyed him. "I didn't figure it was." Adele noticed her hand wandered to a box of bright stones sitting on the counter. She had never seen the woman so nervous.

The sheriff seemed to notice this too, as he removed his hat and took her hand. His tone was soft and gracious. "My mother was telling me the other day how much she needed your excellent twine for some old letter boxes she has in the attic."

"Well, I just got me more from the good lady here." The

woman pointed a wrinkled finger at Adele.

"You go around and see her next week, then," he said.

"I'll do that little thing."

"We have some questions for you," he continued, more business-like. "You know there have been some thefts in the area recently?"

"Heard about that," she mumbled, leaning against a three-legged table.

"I told you." Nin nudged her friend. "Ask her how she heard about it."

"Someone should keep that cat quiet," Zephyr spit out. "Ain't got no business putting her nose into other people's affairs."

Hatfield watched as Zephyr playing with the stones. "I am asking you, though."

The blond woman gave a short laugh. "Well, I tell you, Sheriff, I was down in Blue Springs one day. Had a couple people buying off a china set I got hold of for a song."

"Yes?"

"Bitty pieces, you know, people that don't got the high and mighty stuff like Mrs. Faderman —"

"Just stick to the facts, Mrs. Brown," Jackson interrupted, winning a glare from his sister.

"I heard about a pair of earrings that went missing from a jewelry store down there," she said. "Love-knots, they call them. What a name!"

"When was this?" asked the sheriff.

She flicked her head back. "Oh, a couple of months ago, maybe."

"A few months!" Jackson looked at Hatfield. "Our list only covers last month."

"And you didn't think to tell us?" the sheriff eyed her.

"What the blazes for?" she snapped. "Told you, I don't go poking my nose into other people's business like *some* people." She glared meaningfully at Nin.

"The sheriff is responsible for the entire county," said Nin. "Of course it's his business."

"Guess I didn't think about that," Zephyr grumbled.

Hatfield made a face as if he weren't surprised. "So now we may add earrings to the list, Jackson."

"Probably more once we hear what Edison found out when he questioned the store owners here," Jackson said.

"Or when you question her more," Nin insisted. "I think she has something to hide."

"Careful you don't get fleas when the cat scratches, I always say." Zephyr gave Nin a staunch look.

"What is it you think she's hiding, Miss Branch?" asked Hatfield.

"A gang of thieves," Nin answered. "It wouldn't be the first time. Would it?" She glared at Zephyr.

"Ridiculous!" Adele couldn't hold back.

"Is it, Del?" asked her brother.

Zephyr was very serious when she answered, "I never gave the police any reason to chase me, Deputy. That's the truth. I keep as far away from the law as possible."

"Even when you have information that could help them," Hatfield said dryly.

"Didn't stop to think them earrings in Blue Springs were connected to rumors about a thief in the area, Sheriff. Honest." This came out in a sheepish voice.

"Why weren't those earrings on our list, sir?" Jackson asked.

The woman gave a cackling laugh. "Doesn't surprise me they weren't. Deputy there's kind of lumpy, if you know what I mean. But I haven't heard nothing more about these thefts that could help you."

The sheriff seemed satisfied with this, but it was clear Jackson wasn't through with her. "What time did you go to my sister's shop?"

"After lunch sometime. Must have been about one-thirty or so."

"How do you know it was one-thirty?"

"Got this devil of a cuckoo I been hauling around that I've been trying to get rid of for weeks," Zephyr said. "Hollers every thirty minutes. You wouldn't be looking to buy a clock for that dear mama of yours, now, would you, Sheriff?" She gave him a toothy smile.

"Miss Branch was the only one in the shop when you arrived?" Jackson didn't even try to conceal the impatience in his voice.

"Weren't no one there," she said. "That cat must've seen me coming and run like the devil."

Nin's eyes flashed as she pressed her fists together.

"How long was it before my sister came back?"

"Well, the cuckoo didn't holler, so probably not thirty minutes."

"Thirty minutes," Jackson mused. "That would have been enough time."

But Hatfield was clearly not ready to go that route, as he gave his deputy a silencing look. "Have you seen or heard anything around town today you think we need to know about?" he asked. "Someone who might have had an attraction to pens, for example?"

"Adele didn't find that ugly thing?" Zephyr shook her head. "Thought it might be somewhere in her shop. Things were kind of a mess."

"But you would know if anyone came in before you?"

"We've been through that already, Sheriff." Adele stepped forward. "Nin was in the back when Zephyr came into the shop, and no one came in before her."

"So she claims." Nin followed close behind her.

"I believe her, Miss Branch," said Hatfield. "Mrs. Brown has too much respect for your friend not to tell all she knows." Adele smiled. "What about the rest of the day, Mrs. Brown? No suspicious strangers?"

"Most everyone's suspicious in my part of town," she said.

"Mr. Sipes, for example?" Jackson asked. "The man with the golden cat."

"Gold is infinite," Adele mused.

"Beg pardon?" Zephyr turned to her.

"Nothing important." She blushed.

The blond woman shrugged and turned back to the sheriff. "He and his feline were doing tricks last night for the young ones in Quarry Lane. He used a whip on it. I kind of got the feeling he ain't been handling the animal for very long."

"He made it seem as if he and Sinbad have been together for years," Adele mused.

"Where were they doing these tricks?" asked her brother.

"Near the old barn behind the saloon," she said. "Got some friends in town put up a bed for him there, or so he says."

"Make a note of that, Jackson," said the sheriff.

"Now, mind, I ain't accusing him," Zephyr said quickly. "We got to talking. His daddy was a silver miner like me. Had a mine not far from where mine was, in fact. He was a Silverite too."

"Silverite?" Adele asked.

"Haven't you ever heard of them, honey?" Zephyr's hat had flopped down near her eyes so Adele could hear her voice plainly but not see more than her chin. "They're fighting the gold standard like hell — beg your pardon." She grinned, catching Jackson's stern look. "But you know when big business gets its claws into the government —"

"You seem to know quite a lot about silver and gold for one who doesn't own much of anything, Mrs. Brown," Jackson remarked.

Adele glared at him. "It's not like you to be so insensitive, Jack."

"I don't mind it." Zephyr grinned. "I always loved the white over the yellow, if you know what I mean. My mine was a tiny one. It just ran dry, as mines do."

"Is that what happened to Mr. Sipes?" Hatfield leaned against a few chairs stacked in the corner that looked none too steady.

"He didn't say," Zephyr said. "I know his daddy and a bunch of others went to Sacramento to ask the government to let silver in for trade in these parts. Of course they didn't get anywhere."

"Did you talk to Mr. Fields too?" asked Jackson.

"Who?"

"The gentleman in a wrinkled suit," Adele said. "He thought you were a suspicious person when he saw you come into the shop."

"He the one that don't like young men in nice dress?"

"I see you heard about his argument with Mr. Lyman." The sheriff smiled.

"Heard nothing."

"You who sees everything and knows everything?" Nin asked with a smirk.

Zephyr ignored her. "I was bargaining with Mr. Moffitt over some wires, and this man got into a fight with one of Percy Faderman's pals."

"It seems our Mr. Fields enjoys a good argument," Jackson said dryly.

"No, Deputy, this was an out-and-out fight. Yelling and calling names. Not very dignified." She raised her chin at the last.

"I wouldn't think you would know much about dignity," Nin said with the same smirk. The older woman glared.

"What was the fight about?" asked the sheriff.

"Cuff links."

Hatfield shot Jackson a look.

"They were nice, but not worth the fight, I'd say."

"Thank you, ma'am." Hatfield bowed and put his hat on. "Can we escort you to the picnic?"

"That ain't the place for me, Sheriff," she said. "I'm going to livelier digs. The saloon has a picnic of its own." She winked.

"We'll leave you to it, then." As she was putting on her hat, he stood in the doorway, blocking it with his massive figure. "Before you go, I need a promise from you, Mrs. Brown."

"I'm not so good at making promises, Sheriff." She looked at him shifty-eyed.

"You'll make this one," he said, his voice firm. "Anything of a criminal nature, no matter how big or small, you come tell us about it, and we promise not to assume anything. If we hear about it later, we will start assuming. Understand?"

Zephyr sighed. "You drive a hard bargain, but I guess I never shied away from no bargaining. Ta-ta!" She waved her fingers as she trudged down the gravel street.

"Ta-ta!" Nin snarled. "Who does she think she is, one of Mrs. Faderman's geese?"

The sheriff roared with laughter and shook out his hat before putting it on. "I think it's about time we started having a little of the holiday, don't you, Jackson?" He eyed his deputy.

"I've been looking forward to it, sir," he said with a smile.

"May I?" Hatfield held out his arm to Adele.

"I'm afraid I'm not quite ready yet," she admitted, feeling a little shy. "My dress is grainy from the walking and, well, I'd rather go home first and change."

"You look perfectly fine to me, Del," her brother grumbled.

"Even I have my pristine moments, Jack," she retorted. "You're not the only Gossling to be concerned with his appearance."

"Dandified is more like it," Nin mumbled.

Her brother stiffened and looked down at his immaculate suit, shifting his walking stick to one side.

"I'm not dressed either," Nin added. "I'm sure Mrs. Faderman would kick me out if I came like this." She spread her skirt a little. She was wearing one of her free-flowing dresses and her hair was only half pinned up.

"It's settled then," Adele said. "Nin and I will meet you in the park entrance. We'll try not to be too long."

"I've yet to see you spend over ten minutes on your attire," Jackson said with a wink at the sheriff.

"You should be grateful for that, Jack." She spun around with a satisfied look on her face.

She left Nin to climb the steps of her flat above her store and walked home. To her surprise, Tomas and Ruth were still there, their children fluttering around with excited murmurings in English and Spanish.

"Why aren't you at the picnic, Ruth?" she asked.

"Señorita, we start to go but a man come."

"A man?"

"Small man with big animal," Tomas said, his face looking gaunt.

"Small man with —" She stopped, her blood running cold. "Mr. Sipes!"

"He say you have his card," said Ruth.

"What did he want?" She clutched the bannister.

"He say he want to show you his cat's tricks," said the woman.

"He nice man," said Tomas with a big grin. "He see you not here so he show Marco and Ana his cat's tricks. Even Pilar clap her hands, sí?" He glanced at his middle daughter who gazed with her lovely green eyes, nodding vigorously.

"I see." Adele blinked. "Thank you for telling me. And please, go to the picnic. This day is for you too." She smiled at them.

Tomas bowed, and Ruth gave her one of her serene smiles. She heard them scurrying out as she reached her room.

She dressed quickly, her fingers plucking at the buttons and her combs almost ripping through her hair as she swept it up. She hurried back to Bridge Street, finding Nin waiting for her outside her shop.

"Nin! He tried to see me again."

"He?"

"Mr. Sipes."

"The arrogance of the man!" her friend growled as they began walking toward the park.

"He came by the house," said Adele, taking her friend's arm.

"What for?"

"To show me his cat's tricks, he said." Adele stared into the distant blue sky. "I wonder."

"He was teasing you," Nin insisted. "Trying to frighten you again."

"I don't think so," she said.

"I think we ought to tell the sheriff," said her friend. "That cat of his is dangerous and he shouldn't go gallivanting around town with it."

Adele nodded, lost in thought.

~~~~~

The afternoon heat rose as they reached Arrojo Park. Jackson and the sheriff were waiting for them near the gate. Her brother had a large leaf in his hand and was brushing the red powder dust from his shoes. "We've eliminated all the suspects we had, sir," he said. "It looks like we're back to where we started."

"If our thief is a stranger," Hatfield said, "you and I both know how complicated it will be to catch him."

"Edison may have news for you," Adele suggested.

"Provided his common sense wasn't clouded by hot dogs and summer bonnets," Hatfield snarled.

"If the appearance of Mr. Sipes at Adele's house is anything to go by, I'd say you're being optimistic, Sheriff," Nin remarked.

"What!" Jackson was all attention. "He came to see you, Del?"

"He came to the house," she said.

"How the devil did he know where to find you?" Hatfield snarled.

"It's not difficult in a town like this to find an address, Sheriff," Adele said.

"The man probably double-talked Mr. Duncan into giving it to him," Nin snarled.

"Even the town's postmaster has his limitations, Miss Branch," said Jackson. "It would have been unseemly of him to give our address to a stranger."

"I mean to give Edison a heavy talking-to for not running the man out of town like I told him," Hatfield growled.

"Maybe it was better he didn't, sir," Jackson said. "He might still end up on our list of suspects."

"Even if he were, some people in town would complain you weren't doing your duty by suspecting a stranger," Adele said.

This remark made her brother give her a sharp look. "Those aren't the people whose good opinion concern us, Del," he said.

"You didn't hear what Mrs. Faderman had to say this afternoon."

"We can hardly run an investigation to please her," Jackson retorted.

"But you can't deny, Jack, her opinion counts in Arrojo."

Hatfield glanced at her. "I've always done things my way, Adele, and I've a record of success. I'm happy to show it to Mrs. Faderman or anyone who cares to see it."

"I don't think Adele needs convincing, sir," Jackson said in a light voice.

"No," she said firmly. "I don't."

Hatfield relaxed, the boyish features returning to his face.

And yet, Adele couldn't stop thinking about the argument she had with Mrs. Faderman. When Jackson and Hatfield were well ahead of them, she said to Nin in a low voice, "I have to tell Mrs. Faderman the patrol was my idea."

Nin glanced at her. "It can hardly matter now."

"But it does," said Adele. "The sheriff is worried. I can tell."

"You spar with her all the time," her friend pointed out.

"It wasn't just sparring this time, Nin," she said. "I was scratching at the surface of her impeccable reputation and she didn't appreciate it."

"Don't listen to Zephyr," Nin snorted. "She has no more

standing in Arrojo than a flea."

"Neither have I," Adele said with a small smile. "But it isn't about social standing. It's about pride. 'Pride goeth before destruction.'"

"She ought to examine her own pride before she goes putting down others,'" Nin said with narrow eyes.

"Maybe I ought to as well," Adele said softly.

"You've done nothing to be ashamed of," said her friend in a fierce voice.

She felt her cheeks flush at the memory of the street scene. "What about the bumbling patrol?"

"That was the fault of those silly boys, not you," Nin reminded her.

"There's something I haven't told you, dear." She pressed her friend's hand. "I exposed her."

Nin looked interested.

"I told everyone she kept the council from warning people about the thefts."

"You told the truth, then," Nin insisted.

"An unpleasant truth." Adele shifted her parasol to the other side, glad for its sturdy stick. "One I had no business telling."

They had reached the park. The diamond-shaped grass gave an air of calm and freshness that contrasted the red dirt roads she was used to in Arrojo. A path of gray and white stone criss-crossed the center where a fountain of a California grizzly bear spurt forth water for horses and children. Missy told her Mrs. Faderman had donated it. The animal towered above the shivering small trees much like its donator did over the ladies in town.

"It seems Mrs. Faderman not only has town pride but state pride as well," she remarked.

"'Pride goeth before destruction,'" Nin said.

People sat on the grass near or around the fountain. Men cooked the meat over a fire, and women tended children and picnic food. Dogs ran everywhere. She suddenly missed the Labor Day picnics in Golden Gate Park where different groups displayed their way of celebrating the holiday. Here, it was all on one note, as if the many faces she saw belonged to the same family tree.

Nin was clearly uncomfortable, and Adele felt her hand press hard into her arm. Her friend preferred her own company and exposing herself to the townspeople always meant stares and hushed voices falling after her as she passed.

"I promised Ma to take the meat to the fire, but I must find Edison," Hatfield said. "I'm afraid I'll have to ask you to go instead, Jackson."

"Of course, sir," he said. "I'll send Lady Augusta your apologies while you pursue this investigation."

"Even a lawman has a right to his holiday, Sheriff," said Adele in a soft voice.

"He might have vital information that can't wait, Del," her brother insisted.

"Ma knows the nature of this work," Hatfield said.

It was Nin who spoke up. "Lady Augusta was complaining this morning how she rarely sees you except to say good morning."

Adele immediately wished her friend didn't have such a forth-right manner. Hatfield's forehead wrinkled, and he looked genuinely disturbed. He dipped his hat and quickly disappeared into the crowd.

"You needn't have reminded him of the consequences of his duty, Miss Branch," Jackson said.

"Perhaps it does some good to remind him now and then, for Lady Augusta's sake," said his sister.

Just then, she spotted Mrs. Faderman. The woman was in her element, playing the good hostess with a bottle of wine in one hand and a pitcher of lemonade in the other. Her pince-nez swung back and forth around her neck as she bent down to pour the drinks and chatted with people in a much friendlier way than any other day of the year.

Adele's stomach tightened. She caught Mrs. Faderman's eye and gave her a courteous smile. The woman nodded but did not smile back. It was only when Jackson stooped with a tweak of his hat to give her a bow that she bestowed upon him one of her hostess smiles.

"Good evening, Mr. Gossling." The silver-haired woman returned his bow with a curtsey she had clearly cultivated for such occasions, a little chunky because of the beverages in her hands. "Miss Gossling, Miss Branch." She then moved on to a small circle of people without a further word.

"She doesn't seem inclined to chat with *us*," Nin whispered. "Praise God."

Jackson's hand reached for Adele's. "I can't help but agree, Miss Branch, though I might have said it more delicately."

"You know I don't prettify my words, Mr. Gossling," she answered. "A quality I know your sister appreciates even if you don't. Isn't that true, Adele?"

She hardly heard her. The desire to confront Mrs. Faderman was too strong and without a word, she slipped her hand out of her brother's, picked up the train of her skirt and marched into the crowd.

Mrs. Faderman whirled around. Her face, though stoic, was not sour or vicious. "Is there something you wanted, Miss Gossling?"

"I wanted to apologize." Adele pressed her hands together in what she hoped looked convincing as a gesture of supplication. "You were right about Assistant Deputy Edison and the others. They were incompetent for the task they were given."

"I'm glad you agree," she said. "Now, is there anything else?"

The disconcerting voice brought back a little of Adele's courage. "I also wanted to apologize for what I said this afternoon."

"Oh? What did you say?"

Adele stiffened as she realized the woman was deliberately pretending she didn't remember. "It wasn't my place to say anything about the council's decision, since you seem to believe it was made in the best interest of the community."

"As we all believed?" The woman's eyebrows arched.

"All right. What *was* in the best interest of the community," Adele mumbled.

The woman's hostess smile came out at last. "I accept your apology, Miss Gossling." She stuck out her hand which Adele took and gave it a brisk shake.

"Please don't blame the sheriff for Edison's mistake about Mr. Raleigh's uncle. He isn't to blame, you see." She pressed her hands together again. "It was my idea."

Mrs. Faderman set the wine bottle and pitcher down on the grass. "Miss Gossling, you're quite confusing today. *What* was your idea?"

"I was the one who suggested Sheriff Hatfield send out Edison and the other assistant deputies."

Mrs. Faderman sighed. "I came to *that* conclusion this morning."

Adele winced. "It was my mistake and no one else's. I'm sure you'll agree there's no need to go to the council with any disparaging remarks about the sheriff, since he had nothing to do with it."

Mrs. Faderman bent down, straightening the lemonade pitcher that had begun to tilt a little in the uneven grass. "I'm afraid I don't, Miss Gossling."

Adele dropped her hands, feeling them dampen inside the lace gloves.

"Your idea, though well intended, was misguided." She looked at her squarely. "As I see it, the sheriff made a much bigger mistake by following your advice."

Adele stared at her. "You can't mean that!"

"A man with his years of experience allowing a young woman, especially one with radical ideas, to advise him is questionable at best," the woman said coldly. "At worst, I don't dare say."

Adele flushed. "So you're going to get revenge on me because of what I said this afternoon through him. Is that it?"

"I'm only concerned with the good of this community."

Adele eyed her. "Just how concerned are you, Mrs. Faderman?"

"Enough so that I *might* bring it up at the next board meeting." Here, she picked up the wine bottle and pitcher, indicating the discussion was over.

But Adele was hardly ready to drop her guns. She leaned her head back and examined the woman, a trick she had learned from her suffragist friends to bring down arrogance. It didn't seem to work with Mrs. Faderman.

"Would you be less concerned if he produced the thief who's been plaguing this county for months?"

"If it were within the next twenty-four hours, I'll consider his judgment sound to my satisfaction." The woman nodded. "I'm sure the board would agree with me."

"Because you would make them agree?"

"Because I would make them agree."

This affirmation was so uncharacteristically bald of Mrs. Faderman that Adele was left open-mouthed as she watched her go back into the crowd with the wine bottle and pitcher.

She saw her brother standing with Nin near a tree. "Jack!"

They both turned around with alarm.

"We must help Sheriff Hatfield find the thief *today!*"

"We?" He looked at her sharply.

She glared at him. "I said *we* and I meant it."

"I thought *we* have been doing nothing else for the last few hours."

"This is no joke, Jack." She plucked at the button on his sleeve. "It may very well mean his job."

"Is that what that harpy told you?" Nin asked.

Her brother's strong arm went around her shoulder as when they were children and she had fallen on the ground during playtime. "No one is going to fire the sheriff."

"*She* will," Adele insisted. "If only to spite me."

"You're exaggerating, dear sister," he sighed. "It's hardly becoming."

"I'm not exaggerating. She has reason for spite," she said. "I told everyone about the thefts."

"Del! You promised!"

"It was in a misguided moment of righteousness," she admitted.

"More like a thoughtless moment of temper tantrum!"

"That woman was attacking her!" Nin insisted. "What would you have done?"

"I would have smiled, bowed, and walked away with dignity and grace, Miss Branch," he said in a stiff voice.

"How terribly *manly* of you." Nin's shrill voice made the couple passing by look at them with alarm.

"I would be obliged if you would keep your voice down," Jackson mumbled.

"She all but admitted it, Jack," Adele continued in a hushed voice. "Unless the sheriff brings in the thief within twenty-four hours, Mrs. Faderman will have him fired."

"Even Mrs. Faderman wouldn't have the power to do that."

"She'll make a damn good try of it," Nin said. He winced at her harsh language.

"I thought you liked the sheriff," Adele shot out.

He took her hand between both of his. "Sheriff Hatfield is one of the most trustworthy lawmen I've ever encountered. He won't fail to find the thief."

"Within twenty-four hours!"

"We will do our best. I see Lady Augusta is waiting for us." He lifted his cane and waved.

"We have to help him if he's to bring in the thief in a day," she insisted.

"Considering the damage you've done already, I advise you to stay out of it, Del," said Jackson. "Let us do our work."

Her chest heaved as he strolled in the direction of the platform where Lady Augusta and Rowena sat waiting for them.

"You're not going to give up, are you?" Nin took her arm.

"Of course not," Adele said. "Jack may not take Mrs. Faderman seriously, but I do."

"It's more than Mrs. Faderman now, isn't it?" Nin asked.

Adele stared at her. "What do you mean?"

Her friend grinned mischievously. "There are auras of affection between you and the sheriff, aren't there?"

"Oh, don't be silly!" Adele yanked her forward. "I simply don't believe it's right to let a decent man lose his job for my errors in judgment."

Lady Augusta and Rowena had stationed themselves on the wooden platform in the corner of the park. The elderly woman had changed into a cotton dress with tiny roses and donned a hat with a red sash around the brim. Rowena sat beside her in a wide-brim hat and sleeves covering her wrists as if she were afraid of the sun. Jackson was searching the baskets under Rowena's disapproving eye. Lady Augusta, too, looked far from pleased.

"It's a shame, and I will make that clear to Horatio when he comes!"

Adele exchanged a glance with Nin. She had never heard the noble woman speak with such harshness toward her son.

"He had important police business to attend to, ma'am." Jackson gently took the basket Rowena held in her hands in a rather possessive way. "He never would have asked me to take his place otherwise."

The elderly woman clucked her tongue. "He promised me he would forget his work tonight. That's why I insisted he take care of the meat." She sighed. "I wish you would speak to him, Adele."

"What can I do?" She stared at the woman.

Lady Augusta regarded her with sparkling blue eyes. "You could do a world of good for him if you chose."

Adele glanced over the rail of the platform, hoping her flushing cheeks did not show in the brilliant sun. She saw Edison between tall hats belonging to a group of ladies, but she quickly lost sight of him.

"I'm afraid even Del's charms couldn't persuade him today," said Jackson with a respectful bow.

Lady Augusta sighed. "I warned him too much would be expected of him if he took the job as county sheriff."

"It's others who have unrealistic and unfair expectations." Adele could hardly hold back her anger.

"Others who have no authority over the law," Jackson insisted.

"They think they do, Jack, even if they don't deserve authority over a dog!" his sister retorted.

"Pity you didn't consider that this morning," he murmured.

The shame she felt walking away from the moveable tea party that afternoon returned. "We all make mistakes even when our hearts are in the right place. The important thing is to correct them if we can."

"I couldn't agree more." Lady Augusta patted Adele's hand. "I much prefer your well-placed heart over Irene's mistaken sense of authority."

"Ladies who have a straight nose see clearer the crookedness of men," said Rowena with a nod.

"Shall I bow to you and say, 'What would the police do without you?'" Jackson asked.

"You needn't be sarcastic," Nin snapped.

"We've only been trying to help," Adele murmured.

"That *we* again," Jackson mumbled. "It's making me uncomfortable."

"No one ever died from discomfort, Mr. Gossling," Nin said with ease. "If anything, they grow from it."

He glared at her. "I thought five-foot-eleven was enough growth for any man, Miss Branch." Then he left, his footsteps pounding the wooden stairs as he headed for the fires, making the platform rattle.

"I can't appreciate your brother's sense of humor, Adele." Nin glared after him.

Lady Augusta patted her hand. "You mustn't mind him, dear. He's one of the few who appreciates Horatio's dedication."

Adele sat down beside her. "I didn't mean to bring about unpleasantness."

"It seems as if unpleasantness has been in the air all day," said the woman. "My son went chasing after it."

"Criminals don't sleep a wink in the dust," Rowena added.

"Neither do town meddlers," Nin said.

Lady Augusta glanced at Adele. "So Irene is up to her old tricks again, eh? I thought that was who you meant."

Adele reached for Nin's hand and gave it a discreet squeeze. The last thing she wanted was for the elderly woman to know of the peril that threatened her son.

"Lady Augusta," she said, "you saw nothing strange or off when you were in town today, did you?"

She grimaced. "My dear, to an old woman like me who prefers the sanctuary of her garden to the city street, everything looks strange or off."

"But you're a woman of the world," Adele said. "Surely, if there were something out of place, you would recognize it."

"We weren't in town long enough," she said. "We went straight home when we left your shop. Isn't that so, Rowena?" She threw her head back at her companion, who nodded.

Adele looked at the grass a little distance away, but she saw only blurred green lines. "The sheriff is anxious."

"So are you," Nin said quietly.

"I know he's worried," said Lady Augusta. "He was up at two o'clock this morning devouring the bread and cheese. Horatio has his way with them when he's upset."

Adele tried not to smile. "It's all rather troubling."

"Well, I wish he would forget about it just for today," Lady Augusta grumbled. "Perhaps it's just the thing he needs."

"He oughtn't to worry so much about pleasing the council," Nin said. At Adele's sharp look, she added, "I'm sure he knows to whom his duty lies."

Lady Augusta laughed, and even Rowena chuckled. They exchanged a look that lingered a little too knowingly upon one another as they each picked up a fan and began generating as much wind as they could on that scorching afternoon.

"Did I say something funny?" Nin asked, blinking with genuine innocence.

"Horatio has always done his duty at the cost of his own pleasure in life," said the older woman.

"By work alone a man's soul withers," said her companion.

"You've found some poetry in you for a change, Rowena." Lady Augusta's eyes twinkled. "That proves you're as romantic as they come, just as I've always suspected."

"You're not implying romance has anything to do with it?" asked Nin.

"Perhaps you ought to ask your friend," said Lady Augusta. "You're unusually quiet, my dear, for one so outspoken."

"Saucy-speak, I call it," Rowena declared.

"There's nothing wrong with sauciness in the right direction," her mistress said, "but it mustn't lead one to a broken heart."

Adele realized what she had been hinting at and understood the looks exchanged between the two older women. She rose. "Lady Augusta, I have the deepest regard for your son as the sheriff of this town. That's all."

"I've been telling her all along that he's sweet on her," Nin said.

The bald statement sent both the older women into another peal of laughter.

Adele grabbed her purse and reached inside for a handkerchief, more for something to keep her hands steady than anything else. "My work is my shop, and Sheriff Hatfield's duty lies — well, in his duty."

"Naturally, dear," said Lady Augusta. "But duty and love need not have any bearing on one another."

"Even so," Adele felt genuinely flustered, "I ask that we drop the subject."

"Now you're behaving like the saucy girl we know," Rowena said with approval.

She was relieved to see Edison and waved at him. "The sheriff is looking for you, Assistant Deputy!"

"Yes, I know," he said. "That is, I guessed, well, I saw —"

"You've seen him already?"

"No, miss," he said with a sheepish grin. "That is, I spotted him, but he went in the other direction."

"You mean you hightailed it in the other direction." Nin eyed him.

"Mr. Edison," Lady Augusta said in a tight voice, "am I to understand you're avoiding my son?"

"Well, I wouldn't go so far as to say that, ma'am."

"He's afraid of another tongue-lashing like the one he got this afternoon." Nin grinned.

Adele felt compassion for the young man's quivering hands as he rubbed them together. "Why don't you join us?"

"No thank you, miss," he said. "I got — I have a message. For the sheriff."

"You have something to report?" She leaned over the railing.

"I suppose you could say that, miss."

"Well, don't be pigeon-livered about it," Nin snapped.

"If you've a message for him, shouldn't you look for him?" Lady Augusta asked.

"Got rocks in his shoes, that one," Rowena said.

"I guess I ought to," he mumbled, turning around.

Adele could see the young man was sincerely afraid he would receive more than just a tongue-lashing. She felt guilty that, with her story of Mr. Sipes's visit to the house, she would provide it if the sheriff caught him.

"I'll give him your message," she said, descending the wooden stairs. "You deserve to enjoy the picnic after your hard day's work."

"I'm afraid Mrs. Faderman didn't think much of it," he said.

"Don't you mind Irene, young man." Lady Augusta turned her chair around. "She barks, but she rarely bites. It's Horatio you should worry about."

"I am, ma'am. Believe me, I am." His neck stretched so tight that the veins showed.

"Perhaps it's just as well we surprise him with some good news, then," Adele said. "I assume you have good news?"

"You're very kind, miss," he said. "You've always been kind to me."

"Careful, young man," Lady Augusta snapped. "Don't go making too much of your gratitude."

"No, ma'am. Oh, no, ma'am, I wouldn't think of it!"

Adele smiled. "You've done me a good turn more than once, and I'm happy to return the favor."

"A good turn?"

"You let her take evidence out of the police station," Nin reminded him.

Adele gave her friend a look. "What is it you wish me to tell the sheriff?"

"Well, miss," he said. "Me and the assistant deputies, we did as we were told."

"Ordered, you mean," Nin said.

The young man blushed.

"You talked to everyone?" Adele said.

"Everyone we could find."

"And?" She raised her parasol.

"They don't know nothing — anything."

"Not a thing?"

"So they say," he mumbled.

"You think some of them aren't telling the truth, Assistant Deputy?" Adele eyed him. "Come now, we trust one another, don't we?"

He shrugged. "My job is to ask questions, miss, not speculate. The sheriff's told me that often enough."

Lady Augusta chuckled. "Horatio can be a little like a firecracker fuse, Mr. Edison. His snap and crackle is as harmless as Mrs. Faderman's bark."

"I know that, ma'am." He bowed.

She patted the young man's shoulder. "Remember how we had a suspicion during the Marsh case about the teacup and we proved it right?" She tried to ignore Nin's incredulous look. "I trust your judgment as much as you trust mine, Assistant Deputy."

Edison's face turned almost purple. "We were right about that, weren't we, miss?"

"Indeed we were," Adele said. "And I'm sure you've a good hunch this time as well, but I need to know what it is."

"I'll do anything I can, miss," he said. "I — well, I suppose I bumbled badly today."

Adele flinched. "We all did, Assistant Deputy. Now we must make it right."

"Yes, miss." He stood a little taller, ready for duty.

"You say people around town *say* they saw nothing suspicious," Adele continued. "Do you believe them?"

"Well, miss," he took on an exaggerated air of authority, "they insist they were too busy looking for bargains and there were too many visitors in town. Now, in my experience —" Nin spit out a laugh, "— in my experience, people don't go around looking for something they ain't — aren't expecting, if you know what I mean."

"I know what you mean." She nodded. "So we may assume general bystanders were telling the truth. What did the owners say?"

"None of them admit to having anything taken," he said. "But see here, I don't think they were all telling the truth. It was — well, it was in their faces, miss. And a couple of them couldn't look me in the eye when they said it."

"Very good, Assistant Deputy." Lady Augusta nodded with approval.

"The fox isn't so blind to the henhouse after all," Rowena remarked.

"What about Mr. Ellingsworth?" Adele asked. "He was the one who went to the police."

"He wouldn't admit to going to the post office," Nin growled. "The man thinks everything he does is sacred."

"I didn't ask him, miss," Edison admitted. "I thought there weren't — wasn't — any reason to, since the sheriff has him on the list. But he looked sort of —" He blinked.

"Sort of what?" Nin asked. "Don't be skittish, boy."

He jumped. "Well, I guess mortified is the fancy word the deputy would use."

"He would indeed use that word," Adele said, hiding her smile at her brother's preference for big words one had to look up in the dictionary to understand.

"And he was none too cordial to me," the young man finished. "Acted like he barely knew me."

"Is that unusual of him?" Adele asked.

"Well, frankly, yes, miss. His father and my grandfather were forty-niners together." Edison looked down at his shoes. "He saw me when I was a baby."

"Shoved the bottle in your mouth and everything," Nin snorted.

Adele closed her parasol. "He's a friend of the family, then. It does seem odd."

"Yes, miss," said Edison. "He just wouldn't — well, he's always been a decent fellow to me. Stuck up for me sometimes when no one else would."

"Thank you, Assistant Deputy Edison." Adele smiled. "And don't fret about today. You and the other assistant deputies did the best you could. I'll make sure the sheriff knows it."

"So will I, young man," Lady Augusta said in her lofty way. "I still have a little influence with Horatio, I hope."

"We'll tell him you've un-bumbled your bumbling for the day," Nin said with a nasty little smile.

The young man looked confused for a moment. Then, he saluted Adele and Nin, bowed deeply once more to Lady Augusta, and scampered off to the other side of the park where his friends were gathered along with some of the young women who worked in the shops in town.

"He'll be in for another scolding when the sheriff gets hold of him." Nin sat down on the wooden floor, consistent with her custom of avoiding chairs.

"Nothing of the kind, my dear," said Lady Augusta. "Horatio sent him on an errand, and he completed it and reported back. That's all he ever asks of any of the men working under him."

"Maybe they're telling the truth," Nin offered. "Maybe the thief didn't have time to steal from any other shop but yours and his."

"I wonder." Adele put her chin in her hand.

The elderly woman threw it back toward her companion who was setting a blanket with the salads for the picnic. "Rowena, dear, what was it you heard Mr. Raleigh say before we got here?"

"I didn't really hear what he said, ma'am, but I heard how he said it," said the woman.

"Well, how did he say it?" Lady Augusta asked impatiently. "Don't dilly dally, my dear."

"He was shouting at the wind." Rowena arranged the napkins on the blanket, using rocks to keep them from blowing away in the wind.

"He's always complaining," Nin said.

"This wasn't his ordinary complaining, miss," she said. "He was put out more than usual."

"So Mr. Raleigh was put out," Adele mused. "And Mr. Ellingsworth was uncivil toward Edison."

"It wouldn't take much to lose your civility with that bumbling idiot," Nin snorted.

"But one is hardly apt to be uncivil to a young man one knew as a baby," Adele pointed out. "And a young man he's stood up for in the past."

"I think you ought to find out what it's about, Adele." Lady Augusta peered at her.

"They're hardly likely to speak to me." She sighed.

"The thief stole from your shop too," Nin said. "That might soften them."

"You won't have anything to lose by going to them, will you?" the elderly woman asked.

"An early bird might catch the worm but a flock of them is sure to," Rowena advised.

"My dear, that's the first sensible thing you've said all day," her mistress said.

Mrs. Faderman's smug face came into Adele's mind. She snatched up her parasol. "I think we ought to take a walk on that lovely grass, Nin," she announced. "Perhaps we'll find a few wildflowers for Lady Augusta."

The elderly woman smiled. "Nothing like wildflowers to go with one's dinner."

It didn't take them long to find Mr. Raleigh behind the fountain, as they heard his voice well before they caught sight of him.

"He certainly is shouting at the wind," Nin remarked.

They stood a little behind the fountain so they wouldn't be seen.

Peering around the bear statue's massive figure, she saw some of Arrojo's business owners gathered on the grass. All of them looked decidedly uncomfortable. Mr. Smithson, owner of the art gallery in town, picked at a fruit salad while Mr. Starr with his waxy mustache was withering as if a trail of ants had formed on his blanket. Their wives had the complacent look of society ladies used to keeping still on command. The only lady with her mouth open was Mrs. Raleigh, shouting an affirmative "Indeed!" to everything her husband said.

Mr. Raleigh's anger seemed directed toward Mr. Ellingsworth. "If you had been at the board meeting, sir —"

"But I wasn't, was I?" Mr. Ellingsworth grumbled. "No one has seen fit to elect me on the board."

"If it hadn't been for Mrs. Faderman and her good sense —"

"Good sense!" The other man let out a snort. "That good sense of hers caused me to lose a great deal of money today."

"If the mere taking of a few medals constitutes a great deal of money, sir, I shudder to think what sort of business you could be doing."

"Are you questioning my business skills, Mr. Raleigh?"

"No sir. Only your business sense!"

A low chuckle exploded in the group. Mrs. Raleigh looked annoyed. "Indeed! What Ernest says is all true."

"Am I to understand you're casting blame on one whose regard for our community has been nothing but impeccable?" asked Mr. Raleigh.

"If what Miss Gossling said today was true —"

"Never mind what Miss Gossling said!" Mr Raleigh's fists pounded into the air.

"You cannot deny," Mr. Ellingsworth continued, "that had we all known about the thief, we would have taken precautions. We might even have been watchful of one another's wares."

"Might? We would have been, sir!" Mr. Raleigh proclaimed.

"Then what happened to me wouldn't have happened!"

"You see?" Nin whispered.

"And further, that would, I think, have shown more community spirit than keeping it a secret that there was a thief in our midst," Mr. Ellingsworth finished.

Adele was sure Mr. Raleigh would break into a tirade of defense against Mrs. Faderman again. But when he spoke, his voice was soft and humble. "I didn't think of it that way."

Adele took her friend's hand and pulled her toward the group. "I couldn't agree more, sir."

"You speak as if Mrs. Faderman and the board are your enemies," Mr. Raleigh thundered.

"Indeed!" his wife affirmed.

"I never considered her or anyone else in this town my enemy," Adele insisted.

"I'm sure Mrs. Faderman will be glad to hear it, Miss Gossling," said Mr. Raleigh in a dry tone.

"But she did wrong, sir, and so did I," Adele said. "You see, I knew about the thefts long before most of you."

"You ought to have said something, then," Mr. Ellingsworth said in a sour voice.

"I was sworn to secrecy, sir," she said. "I made a mistake, to be sure. Perhaps it would comfort you all to know that my shop was also robbed."

Mr. Ellingsworth collapsed on the grass, as if forgetting about the empty blanket beside him. Mr. Raleigh cleared his throat. "I resent the implication when you say 'also,' Miss Gossling, as if there are many of us."

"Why shouldn't she say it?" Nin snarled. "Hers wasn't the only one and all of you know it."

"I've my business expenses to worry about, just the same as you." Adele sniffed. "A stolen pen is a stolen pen."

"Just as a stolen medal is a stolen medal!" The antique dealer glared at Mr. Raleigh.

Mr. Raleigh was silent for a moment. "As, I suppose, a stolen thimble is a stolen thimble."

There was a small gasp from the group, and Mrs. Raleigh looked down at the grass as if she had been disgraced.

"Maybe Edison wasn't bumbling for once," Nin mumbled.

"A thimble went missing from your shop?" Adele was immediately alert.

Mr. Raleigh spoke with trepidation. "Well, to tell the truth, several thimbles were nicked."

"Nicked?" Nin inquired.

Mr. Smithson, a stickler for proper grammar, winced. "He means taken."

"How do you know they were nicked?" Adele asked.

"Well, they weren't there when we took inventory, were they, dear?" He glanced at his wife. She nodded, her chins bobbing.

"Were they very valuable?" Adele asked.

"Indeed they were."

"Really?" Nin's eyebrows flew up.

He stiffened. "They were made of pure gold, Miss Branch. That ought to make them valuable enough to catch the eye of any thieving rascal."

Adele's hand pulled at the swan handle of her parasol. "Pure gold?"

"Yes, what of it?"

"Oh, nothing," she said. "My pen was gold as well."

"And my medals were gold!" Mr. Ellingsworth declared.

"An odd coincidence, don't you think?" Adele said.

"Not so odd, perhaps." Mr. Starr cleared his throat. "Properly handled, gold can fetch quite a lot these days."

"Yes, a tidy sum," Mr. Raleigh agreed, sending the gallery owner's countenance in a wince once more. "Gold being what it is."

"Scarce." Adele nodded.

He stared at her. "Are you interested in the market now too, Miss Gossling?"

"Why shouldn't she be?" Nin snapped. "Women know about finance nowadays as much as they do about crime. Of course, we all know what you think about *that*."

Adele squeezed her hand as if to remind her that antagonism would not do for their task at hand. "Was anything missing from anyone else's inventory this afternoon?"

They were all silent, as she predicted. But she could feel an awkward buzz stir, as if some questioned the wisdom of their silence.

She addressed the crowd, "The more the police know about what's been stolen in Arrojo today, the better chance they have of recovering the goods and catching the thief. That's what we all want, isn't it?"

Tension replaced the awkward buzz.

Mr. Smithson was the first to speak. "If you put it that way, Miss Gossling, one of my miniatures seems to have gone astray."

Mr. Moffitt's voice rose next. "So have a pair of cufflinks from my shop."

"What did they look like?" asked Adele.

"Why, they were gold with turquoise inlay."

"Anybody else?"

The crowd remained silent.

"I suppose you're going to tell the police?" Mr. Raleigh eyed her. "It was my understanding you refused to intervene when Mrs. Faderman asked you earlier."

"The situation has altered," Adele murmured.

The man leaned forward. "In what way?"

"That's none of your business," Nin snapped.

He gave her a sneering smile.

"One more thing," Adele said. "Were there any odd incidents or strange visitors in your shops today?"

"Most everyone can look peculiar in the right light, Miss

Gossling," said Mr. Smithson in a breezy tone.

She sighed. "All right. I'll ask the question another way. Did a Mr. Fields visit any of your shops? He was a thin man of middle age in a tweed suit, fond of Revolutionary War relics and not very fond of young men who dress well." She glanced at Mr. Moffitt. "He had an argument over those cufflinks with another man, I was told."

He stared at her like an owl. "How the devil — how in the world did you know that?"

Adele couldn't help but smile. "Let's say a little bird told me."

"A little buzzard named Zephyr," Nin said.

Mr. Moffitt was equally displeased. "I knew I should have thrown that woman out of my shop!"

"I did," declared Mr. Smithson. "I won't have her filthy hands anywhere near my precious works of art."

"Mr. Fields didn't enter your shop?" Adele asked. He shook his head. She turned to Mr. Ellingsworth. "Or yours, sir?"

"The description does sound familiar," he admitted. "I believe there was such a man who examined a scarf rumored to have been left on the battlefield at Eutaw Springs. Of course, I can't be sure."

"Could it be the medals were not in the shop by that time?"

He looked stricken. "I never considered it. Perhaps, perhaps." His head slowly nodded back and forth.

"Don't forget Mr. Sipes and his cat," Nin threw in.

"That abominable man!" Mrs. Raleigh ejaculated

Her husband gave her a silencing look. "Yes, he came into the store."

"And the rest of you?" Adele asked. There were nodding heads all around. "*All* of you?" More nods.

"And he claimed he only patronized exclusive shops," Nin said with a snort.

Adele brushed grass from her skirt. "Thank you all very much. You've all been of immense help."

"Will you now report to your superior, lady detective?" Mr. Raleigh sneered.

"Now, sir. I'm going to do my civic duty. I trust that meets with your approval." She saluted him and her hat shook as a sudden breeze graze it.

The moment they left the group, Adele grabbed Nin's hand and pulled her toward the path. "We must find Sheriff Hatfield. He has twenty-four hours, remember."

Nin glanced at people sitting down to their meals. "We haven't eaten a thing yet."

"What does food matter when a man's career may be at stake?" she snapped.

"I've never seen you so worried." Her friend watched her.

Jackson came toward them with two steaming plates of meat in his hands. He was trying to dodge a small dog whose head almost vanished under the large velvet bow tied around its neck.

"Bother!" he roared.

"You seem to attract many feminine creatures, Mr. Gossling." Nin's smile had a nasty flair to it.

"I assure you, Miss Branch, I wasn't trying to attract this one. Oh, bother!" He tried to sidestep the animal prancing in front of him.

"Jack, have you seen the sheriff?"

"He's with his mother, I expect," he said. "He found out very little, I'm afraid. I suppose it would be too much to ask for a little help?" He thrust a plate at her.

She took it absently. "The sheriff may have found nothing, but we have."

He glanced at her. "I thought we agreed you would stay out of it."

"*You* agreed with yourself," Nin said.

"And what did you find out with your nosing around?" There was a tone of amusement in his voice.

"We'll tell the sheriff only," Nin said with finality.

He growled and gently pushed the dog aside with his foot.

Sheriff Hatfield was on the platform, as she expected, chatting with Lady Augusta while balancing a glass of beer on his knee. He stood on the steps, his bear-like figure domineering and his eyes stormy.

She heard Jackson's voice behind her. "Here's a bite, now will you please go, girl?" The dog gave a whimper.

"Mrs. Faderman's dog is a 'he.'" Lady Augusta wheeled herself to the rim of the platform.

"Mrs. Faderman's dog!" Jackson looked exasperated.

She nodded. "I recognize it by that ridiculous bow. Horatio!" She smacked the edge of her cane against the side of his shoe as she always did when she wanted to get his attention. "Be a gentleman and take the plate from Miss Gossling's hands."

"I was just about to do that very thing, Ma." He lifted the plate heaving with food gently from Adele's hands. "I've been told you're playing detective again."

"We're nothing like that bumbling Edison," Nin defended.

"Then it's true." Although Hatfield had said many times that he welcomed help on investigations when he could get it, he looked less than pleased.

Adele tried to hide her distress. "We asked a few questions, Sheriff. That's all."

"I sent her, Horatio," said Lady Augusta in a firm voice.

"No, I went out on my own," Adele said just as firmly. "We had to do *something*. Mr. Edison found nothing of value in his inquiries."

"How do you know that?"

"Because he was here with his report." Lady Augusta's chin went in her hand, watching them closely. "I told you all about that, Horatio."

"You said Edison was here, but not about his report, Ma." He turned again to Adele. "My guess is that he was looking for me but gave his report to you under your persuasion?"

"He didn't need any persuading," Nin retorted. "He's been fish-eyed about her since she came to town."

"Not to mention he was only too willing to talk to me after you scared the devil out of him this afternoon," Adele retorted.

Hatfield leaned against the stairs. Jackson, clearly uncomfortable at his outspoken sister's outburst, handed his plate to Rowena. The companion tried to get the dog away from him by throwing it a few morsels, but the animal was clearly enamored by its new object of affection.

"You should have sent him straight to me," said Hatfield in a quiet tone. "You realize that."

"The sheriff is right, Del. That wasn't proper procedure." Jackson picked up the dog and deposited him near Lady Augusta's chair. But the animal returned to his side with eager eyes.

"I'm not a member of the police department," Adele said, her shoulders stiffening. "I wasn't aware I was under obligation to follow any procedures."

"Perhaps not," the sheriff agreed, "but you are under obligation as a citizen of this town to let the police handle information pertaining to a case."

Nin eyed him. "You've been grateful for our help in the past."

"That was a different matter," Hatfield said. "Those cases involved a select group of people. This one involves the entire town. I'm inclined to agree with your brother to leave it to the professionals."

"Like Edison and the lads?" Adele asked a tart voice.

"What about the fiasco you had with the ladies this afternoon?" Hatfield dipped his head a little so he could meet her eyes.

"Really, Horatio." Lady Augusta sniffed. "That fiasco, as you call it, was hardly Adele's fault."

Adele glared at him. "Did Jack tell you?"

"He didn't have to. I had a long talk with Mrs. Faderman and a few of the council members." A red flush rose on the sheriff's face.

"Did she also tell you she wants your badge?" Nin asked.

"Nin!" Adele grabbed her friend's hand.

"She didn't come right out and say it, Miss Branch," the sheriff answered. "But she implied she and the council would be most unhappy if we didn't have someone in jail by the end of the day tomorrow."

"Why, that's absurd!" Jackson snarled. "This thief has been at large for months. She can't do a thing and she knows it."

"It's enough that she thinks she can," Lady Augusta said. A troubled look appeared under the wrinkles of her face.

"The bee that stings always leaves its mark," Rowena said.

"What we've discovered might help you, Sheriff," Adele insisted, "if you'll just listen."

Jackson took a place beside his superior, and the dog immediately dove into his lap. "Oh, bother!" He found a pinecone and threw it. The dog darted after it.

Hatfield sighed and sat down on the steps. He took up his pen and pad. "All right. But after this, promise me you'll resign yourself to the celebrations of the day?" His face broke into one of his beguiling smiles.

Though still feeling the sting, she promised and then promptly listed the shops and items, and Nin jumped in with surprising attention to small details, such as the turquoise inlay on Moffitt's cufflinks.

"I saw those cufflinks in the window the other day," Jackson remarked. "Very handsome."

"And very easy to hide when no one is looking," Lady Augusta pointed out. "Everything missing seems to have been easy to hide. Isn't that right, dear?" She glanced at her son.

"Makes sense, Ma," he said. "A thief roaming a busy shop would hardly want to draw attention to himself."

"A man likely to blend into the scenery." Jackson nodded. "A non-descriptive, as the Anspaches used to call them."

The dog came back with the pinecone. Jackson threw it at the fountain, where it promptly fell in with a splash. He burst out laughing as the dog ran after it, dunking its head into the water.

"That was cruel, Jack," said Adele.

"I've no time to play with dogs," he snapped. "We have a thief to catch."

"Mr. Moffitt confirmed Zephyr's story about Mr. Fields arguing with a gentleman over the cufflinks," Adele added. "And Mr. Sipes came to every shop with his cat and his sales speech."

"I'm not surprised," Hatfield said, making a face.

"I was right," Lady Augusta said. "He's a charlatan."

"But hardly a non-descriptive," Adele said in a wry voice. "I wouldn't consider Mr. Fields a non-descriptive either."

"It could have been someone else," Nin pointed out. "I saw quite a few non-descriptive people roaming Bridge Street last night from my window. I could point them out to you if they're here."

"Very good of you, dear," Lady Augusta said with a smile.

"I had some reports of a man with flaxen hair who seemed to eye everything a little too curiously," Hatfield admitted. "That came from one of the lads on patrol."

"Do you think it might be him?" Adele asked.

He glanced at her. "The description fit a man known as Old Bill up and down the county line. He's a vagrant and a drunkard, but he's no thief."

"Perhaps he grew desperate," Jackson suggested.

The dog returned without the dripping pinecone, wagging its tail and awaiting instructions.

Hatfield put his pencil and pad back in his breast pocket. "At least we now know what's been taken in town and from whom."

"You're no longer irked with me, then?" Adele peered at him.

"I suppose one could say the end justified the means," he grumbled. "I only wish we could find a connection between the stolen items. That might help."

Adele poked her fork in the potato salad. "Cufflinks, earrings, thimbles," she mumbled. Her fork fell into the grass. *Gold is infinite.*

"Don't tell me you're developing a woman's fascination with trinkets now, Del." Jackson was amused.

Adele turned to Nin. "Do you remember how taken Mr. Sipes was by my magnifying glass?"

"He was more than taken," said Lady Augusta. "He was spellbound." She glanced at her son. "He insisted Adele remove it so he could scrutinize it."

"Insisted?" Nin snorted. "He bribed her into it. He probably came by your house wanting to get another look at it."

"Mr. Sipes came by your house?" Lady Augusta put her fork down. "How rude!"

Jackson's pleasant face grew vicious. "If I ever see the man again—"

"It is eye-catching," Hatfield admitted. "I've often wanted to have a closer look at it myself."

Adele smiled and slipped the chain from her neck. "You're welcome to it, Sheriff. I've no qualms about giving it to *you*."

Hatfield turned away so quickly that Adele suspected a furious flush had come to his face. "Mr. Sipes said something interesting when he was in my shop," she continued. "Something about the infinity of gold."

"Gold is valuable, just as Mr. Raleigh said," Nin reminded her. "Any thief would know that."

"I'd like to get hold of that quack and give him a piece of my mind," Jackson snarled. "Perhaps a few pieces of my mind." The dog seemed to sense his mounting anger and growled in response. Then, it climbed into his lap and began licking him blind.

"He may not even be in town by now," Hatfield said. "He may have passed your house on his way out. Entertainers come and go through towns like this one very quickly. Most are harmless enough."

"This one isn't," Nin insisted. "I told you, I can feel the man is evil."

"Perhaps it's time to hunt him down and see what he has to say for himself," Adele suggested.

"That's a good idea, dear," said the elderly woman.

"I don't mean to tell you what to do, Sheriff," Adele said, "but with Mrs. Faderman on the warpath —"

"I wouldn't necessarily call it that, Adele," he said.

"But it's close enough." She peered at him. "Can you forgive me?"

"Good heavens, what for?" Lady Augusta stared at her.

"Del thinks she's responsible," said Jackson. "As if the council needed any help finding fault in your methods, sir."

"Or in yours, I daresay," Hatfield remarked. "Lawmen are rarely appreciated for their methods."

A shadow appeared on the wooden floor.

"Are you looking for your dog, Mrs. Faderman?" Adele asked as politely as she could.

The woman twisted her handkerchief in her hands. "Well, as a matter of fact, Miss Gossling, I was looking for you."

"Oh?" Adele stiffened.

"Yes, I — I believe I owe you an apology."

A surprised silence followed.

"You were right about one point," the woman continued. "It was wrong of me to advise the council to keep quiet about the thefts."

"I appreciate and accept your apology, ma'am," Adele said in a kind voice.

"Mr. Raleigh has just told me about the thimble," she said. "He also told me about the other thefts."

Adele said with a smile, "We both made mistakes, I'm afraid."

"I shall be more cautious in the future," she promised. "I trust you will be too?"

"I'll try, ma'am," Adele mumbled.

The woman's confidence return. "I'm glad to hear it."

"Did you *really* think the thefts would never reach Arrojo, Irene?" Lady Augusta inquired, giving her a sharp look.

"Well, ma'am, such a thing as this has never happened in our town," she lamented. "I didn't think we need to worry."

"You didn't *want* to think we needed to worry," Nin snarled.

"You're not to blame, ma'am." Sheriff Hatfield took a light hold of her hand and kissed it. "Just as Miss Gossling isn't to blame. Crime will happen even with the best intentions to prevent it."

There was an awkward silence as the wind cracked against the wooden poles of the platform.

"Well," Lady Augusta said in a booming voice, "I didn't think you had it in you, Irene."

"Never heard of going so far as *that*," Rowena added. "You've done an admirable thing, ma'am."

"Well," she said, squaring her shoulders, "never let it be said of Irene Faderman that she doesn't recognize when she's done wrong." But it was clear she was hardly pleased with these compliments.

"However reluctant a recognition," Nin said with a smirk.

"May I presume, then, you no longer find my son's ethics questionable?" Lady Augusta's head went back, regarding her with the regal, darting eyes people always found intimidating.

The woman shrank back. "I'm sure I implied nothing of the kind, Lady Augusta."

"Adele told us you said you would have him fired if he didn't find the thief in twenty-four hours," Nin said in her blunt way.

"I'm sure Miss Gossling misunderstood me." Mrs. Faderman gave her a cutting glance. "Not that it wouldn't be in the town's best interest to find the culprit as quickly as possible, now that we know he's here."

The dog ran in circles in front of Jackson. He groaned and

held a piece of meat out to the animal, but it backed away from it as if it were poison.

"Otter!" his owner cried, "What on earth is the matter with you?" The animal readily ran to his mistress. "I apologize, Mr. Gossling. Otter is usually such a restrained dog."

"I never found him so," Lady Augusta said in a dry voice.

Adele watched as Mrs. Faderman tied a chain around the animal's neck and began fussing over him. "I can't understand it," she said. "He doesn't take to people, especially men."

"I'm sure I've done nothing to encourage him," Jackson mumbled.

"Why, Otter!" Mrs. Faderman fumbled with the dog. "I believe, Mr. Gossling, this belongs to you?" She handed him a stickpin with three diamonds.

"Otter, you little devil!" Jackson was less than amused as he put the stickpin back in its place in his lapel.

The remark brought back the woman's haughty attitude. "I'll thank you not to insult my dog, sir."

"I apologize, ma'am." He bowed.

She held the pince-nez in place, her hand quivering with disapproval. "Otter was only playing. And as he's taken such a liking to you, I should think you'd be flattered."

At that moment, the sun hit the pin directly. Adele and Nin turned from the glare.

"We would be obliged if you would get those diamonds out of the sun," Nin said.

Mr. Sipes's mesmerizing voice echoed on the wings of a sudden breeze: *Gold is the color of enchantment.*

"It's not the diamonds. It's the gold!" She stared at Otter, now sitting obediently next to his mistress, his tongue out and tail wagging. She sat up on her knees.

"Really, Miss Gossling, that is a most unladylike position," said Mrs. Faderman. "I realize you modern girls take a certain pride in defying manners and good taste, but as the host of this event, I would prefer you maintain some sense of decorum."

"Mrs. Faderman, where did you find Jack's stickpin just now?" she asked, ignoring the reprimand.

"Defying manners and good taste," the woman rattled on, "includes asking indiscreet questions. Most alarming."

"Indiscreet it is, ma'am, but important," Adele said. "Please, where did you find it?"

"On Otter, of course." The woman pulled the dog up by the chain.

"Yes, I know, but *where* exactly?"

"In his mouth, of course." Mrs. Faderman's chin bobbed as it always did when she was preparing to give a lecture. "If you had a dog, Miss Gossling, you would know they often slip things into their mouths. Why, I remember once when Percy was a boy, we had a German shepherd named Earl who used to take his jacks in his mouth and then drop them anywhere. A sort of game they played, I believe."

"Thank you, Mrs. Faderman," Adele said. "Thank you." She sat down with her knees to one side and her skirt generously covering her just as she knew the woman would approve.

When Mrs. Faderman had gone to her other guests, Adele turned to Hatfield. "Sheriff, I think you should locate Mr. Sipes as soon as possible."

"Why the urgency?"

"Because he's responsible for the thefts," she said.

"We have no evidence of that." The sheriff shook his head. "We can't question a man because he's passing through town."

"You can if you have suspicions about him, can't you?" Adele insisted.

"But we don't," Hatfield said. "He may be a charlatan and a rascal, but he's done nothing to prove he's a criminal as well."

"Isn't his roaming about town with a golden tiger suspicious enough?" Nin asked.

"Not if it's his livelihood, Miss Branch," said Jackson. "I'm sure if we were to approach him, he would have papers to show that it is."

"Tigers are dangerous animals," Lady Augusta pointed out. "It could hurt someone."

"You said the cat never even came near you, Ma," Hatfield said.

"He came near me," Nin declared. "He chased me up the counter."

"It's not the tiger, Sheriff," Adele mused. "It's Mr. Sipes and his gold obsession."

The sheriff blinked.

"My sister is talking in circles as usual, Sheriff," Jackson grumbled.

Adele gave him a look and put her plate aside. She had lost her appetite anyway. "It's genuine gold holds a perhaps unnatural fascination for Mr. Sipes, isn't it?"

"Heirlooms fascinate Mr. Sipes, my dear," Lady Augusta corrected. "He told us that himself."

"He lied about that," Adele said.

"Lied?"

"Remember he said he was a great believer in family heirlooms. He meant gold heirlooms!"

"And how do you know that, dear sister?" Jackson eyed her.

"I watched while he examined my magnifying glass," she said. "He hardly touched the glass itself. He was only interested in the casing. And he seemed to know things about it even I didn't know."

"He knew who the maker was," said Nin.

"Precisely," Adele said. "I'm willing to wager if we made a call to Korbo & Sons, they would recall selling my father the magnifying glass. It's not exactly a common piece."

Jackson was quiet for a moment. "You needn't call them.

Father took me to their shop once. They remembered him, and they remembered the magnifying glass they sold him."

Adele jumped. "Mr. Sipes said Papa had foresight giving it to me because of the value of gold on the market nowadays."

"I thought that was odd," Lady Augusta said.

Adele turned to Nin. "Remember what Mr. Starr said about gold?"

"'Properly handled, gold can fetch quite a lot these days,'" her friend imitated the man's arrogant manner, making Sheriff Hatfield roar with laughter.

But Adele didn't laugh. With a thoughtful expression, she said, "I don't think fetching quite a lot was what Mr. Sipes had in mind."

"What do you mean, dear?" Lady Augusta asked.

"I'm not sure," she admitted. "I've a feeling I can't place."

"Next you'll be having auras like your friend, Del," Jackson said. He was rewarded with a seething look from Nin.

"All right," the sheriff sighed. "Gold fascinates Mr. Sipes. But it doesn't follow he stole the items."

"They all contained gold," Adele insisted. "Even the ones stolen in other towns. Look at your list, Sheriff."

Hatfield pulled from his pocket a frayed copy of the list. He bent over one of the candles Rowena had lit and skimmed it, then handed it to Jackson.

"Maybe Del is right, Sheriff," her brother said slowly. "If we find Mr. Sipes, we'll find the missing items."

"He may be miles away by now," Hatfield said.

"He was in town last night," said Adele. "Zephyr said he has friends here, remember?"

"And he was in town just this afternoon," Nin added. "He came to see Adele."

"With that cat of his, I doubt he would get very far anyway," said her brother. "If he's already left town, he may be on the road or even sitting in some jail cell in Finn's Creek or somewhere near here where I'm sure they're less tolerant of strangers than we are, judging from my conversations with the deputies there."

The sheriff rose. "Come, sir, we've work to do." He kissed his mother's cheek. "You stay here with the ladies, Ma."

Both Adele and Nin rose, lifting the edge of their skirts out of the layer of dust on the wooden floor and looking at him expectedly.

"I believe the ladies have made up their minds to accompany you, Horatio," Lady Augusta said with a wry smile.

"After your promise, Del?" Jackson gave her a disapproving look.

"The situation has changed, dear brother," she said. "I was part of the problem before. Now I'm part of the solution."

Sheriff Hatfield grinned. "You're too headstrong for your own good, Adele."

"Perhaps it's a lucky thing for you," his mother snapped. "Every man ought to embrace a headstrong woman. Metaphorically, of course."

"Ma, please." The blush came out again. "Aside from the fact that police business belongs to the police, Mr. Sipes is staying in a part of town where angels, much less ladies, fear to tread."

"But we're treading with the sheriff," Adele said, "and the deputy sheriff. There can hardly be any danger."

"You let us accompany you to the Bright Lights Saloon when we went to see that cowboy," Nin reminded him.

"Perhaps my judgment has become less clouded since then," he said.

Adele caught Hatfield's arm. "Sheriff, I think we should be the ones to speak with Mr. Sipes."

Dimness had fallen over the park. They were illuminated by the candle lights of the platform, a spotlight among the darkened grass where only flickers of single candles shone in the dark.

"Absolutely out of the question!" Jackson roared.

"I think it might be unwise, dear," Lady Augusta said in a soft voice.

"Perfectly incompetent," declared Rowena.

"I must agree with the consensus," said the sheriff. "It might be dangerous, especially with that cat of his."

"That's the whole point," she insisted. "The cat is more amenable to ladies and Mr. Sipes is amenable to his cat."

"He even invited us to come see Sinbad perform," Nin added.

"He stopped by the house to see me especially," Adele pointed out. "If you try to speak with him, Sheriff, you'll get nothing."

"You have a point." Hatfield nodded. "Unless we were to use more unsavory methods that I'm not prepared to use."

"Other police forces do," Jackson murmured.

"*This* police force does not," came back his superior.

Her brother was clearly infuriated by the Hatfield's silence. "You can't seriously be considering this, sir. I won't permit it."

"Adele is over twenty-one," Nin snarled. "She can put herself in the jaws of a tiger if she chooses to."

A burst of laughter emerged from a group not far from them, with two young couples who rose and gathered their things.

Hatfield turned to his deputy. "Bring Edison and the lads. They're somewhere around here. Bring as many as you can find."

Jackson stared at him. "You're going to allow my sister to put herself in danger?"

"I don't intend to let the ladies go it alone," Hatfield said. "We'll be nearby with Edison and the others. Very near."

As Zephyr suggested, Quarry Lane was indulging in even livelier Labor Day celebrations than the more respectable part of town. People caroused around with whiskey bottles in one hand and beer glasses in the other, women kissed men on the street at random, and others had taken up horns and drums and were making enough of a racket to frighten the horses in the street.

Adele had seen enough of such chaotic pleasure-seeking in the Barbary Coast and was neither frightened nor alarmed as reeling men slid glances up and down her tightly gathered figure as she passed. They didn't look twice at Nin, for her gorgon hair and wary eyes stared back at them with a viciousness equal to Medusa.

Mr. Sipes was in the barn behind the Bright Lights Saloon. He had a stall all to himself, but the tiger's cage took up half the small space.

With a cautious nod, the sheriff motioned for Adele and Nin to stop behind the saloon while Jackson dispersed Edison and the other young men, hidden in shadows close enough to be at hand should any trouble begin. Hatfield then motioned for the two women to cross the thorny field to the barn.

Mr. Sipes' reaction proved Adele's hunch right. He immediately rose from the straw bed, smoothing down his hair and clothes. He glanced into the cracked mirror hanging on a peg before he came forward to greet them.

"Why, dear ladies!" He reached out to kiss their hand. Only Adele accepted.

He arranged two crates with a generous cushion of straw for them, though Nin chose the straw on the ground. "Such a surprise!"

Adele could smell a little whiskey about him, but it was clear he was sober. "A pleasant one, I hope, Mr. Sipes."

"Certainly, certainly," the man murmured.

"I've been told you stopped by my house and tried to see me," she said.

"Rather taking liberties," Nin growled.

"Not in the least, my dear woman," he purred. "Your Mr. Duncan at the post office was kind enough to give me your address."

"I shall have a nasty word with him about giving out addresses, then," Nin said.

The man laughed. "You've both come to see my cat do his tricks after all?" He beamed. "Sinbad would be delighted. You're his favorite acquaintances in this town."

"How would you know?" Nin asked. "You've only been in this town a few days."

"Oh, I can tell," he said. "Why, he's like a companion to me."

"A mighty convenient companion with sharp claws and teeth," she snapped.

The man laughed. "Sometimes one needs a more unconventional companion in my profession."

"You chose a strange profession, sir," Adele said.

"One does not choose it." A slight edge came into his voice. "It is one's prophecy."

"I know what you mean, Mr. Sipes," Adele said, patting Nin's hand. "My friend has such a profession. It was handed down to her by her mother. Was yours handed down?"

The man's smile froze as he answered, "My father dealt with his share of wild animals, though not as affable as Sinbad. Now, if you'll step this way, I'm sure we can coax him into showing you some of his tricks."

"We haven't come to see Sinbad, as a matter of fact," Adele said. "We came to see you."

"Oh?"

Adele had been contemplating how she should approach him. As she observed the tiger pacing in its cage in a lethargic way with the gaslight glowing on his golden coat, it came to her. She slipped the magnifying glass from her neck. "I want to sell this, and I need some advice on how much you think it might be worth."

"Adele!" Nin's alarm was genuine as her ungloved hand clutched her friend's arm so hard that Adele could feel her nails digging into it.

"Now, don't try to talk me out of it, dear," she said. "You heard Mr. Sipes this morning. Gold is precious on the market now."

The man's features contorted as if hot wax had been poured over them. In the light, they were almost transparent. "You mustn't do that, dear lady. Keep it and never sell it."

"For the sentimental value?" She eyed him.

"Hang the sentiment!"

Adele thought she heard the shifting of feet outside where she knew the lawmen were stationed. "If not for sentiment, then what?"

"The value of depriving those who use it to cheat people," he said, his eyes glistening. "People who don't have the shrewdness or hard soul needed to fight the mangy dogs." His voice floated in the soft, dim light. "Gold, gold, oh, its cruelty, its devil's play!"

"Mr. Sipes, you yourself told me gold is the color of enchantment," Adele said in a quiet voice.

A ragged laugh escaped his contorted face. "Did I really say that?"

"Those very words," Nin said.

"Cursed. I meant it was cursed."

"Cursed," Adele said. "For men like your father."

"For everyone!"

She clutched her parasol, feeling its tip dig into her hands like a sword. "If gold is cursed, its theft is your vengeance. Yours and your cat's."

Mr. Sipes' face lost its demonic gaze and sagged. He looked at the golden cat that had ceased its pacing and now sat lazily on its haunches in the cage. "Don't blame Sinbad. He's only a dumb animal."

"Mr. Sipes, did Sinbad steal the gold pen with the snakes from my shop?" Adele asked.

The man did not answer, but his head bobbed as if shaken by the ground.

"You taught your cat to steal!" Nin growled. Adele pressed her wrist, and she lapsed back into silence.

"It was quite ingenuous," she said. "The pen was hidden in his mouth when you walked out of my shop, wasn't it?"

The man grinned, showing a sparkle of silver etchings on a few of his teeth. "I told you we do tricks, dear lady. I speak to the people and Sinbad — he does what he feels. Wondrous things, wild beasts." He leaned forward. "They take what they like. They need not be civilized like the rest of us. Even mangy dogs can appear to be civilized. They *relish* civility, all the while clawing and biting and mauling." His eyes became as silvery as his smile.

Adele reached forward and laid her hand on his shoulder. "What have the mangy dogs done to you, Mr. Sipes?"

His eyes were bloodshot as if a burden he had been carrying for years had suddenly filled them. "Not me. My pa, dear lady. An honest, hard-working farmer, he was. Went without to give me the best, even an education."

"It was worth it," she said in a gentle voice. "You speak eloquently, Mr. Sipes."

With a sudden sweeping gesture, the man grabbed her hand and kissed it hard. Nin immediately lunged forward, but Adele held her back.

"What did the mangy dogs do to him?" Adele pressed.

"What do they always do?" Mr. Sipes snarled. "They bought up the shares and drove down the price of wheat and corn and beans."

"So the farmers must go without and more without," Adele said in a soft voice.

The man peered up at her with the eyes of a child. "He lost his farm and then — he lost his mind." He began to laugh, a shrill laugh that bounced around the barn. "He used to say his head was rattling like so many gold pieces. Those greedy, mangy dogs!" The last came out in a blast of fury.

Patches of darkness filtered through the slots of the poorly built barn. The sheriff and his men burst through the door.

Hatfield's voice was hard. "There's no point in playing games with us anymore, Mr. Sipes."

"Games!" the man barked. "The evil of men shines in the eyes of their golden god! Those are the games *they* play."

The sheriff's voice vibrated in the small space and Edison,

who stood beside him, took a step back. "Where is the pen you stole from Miss Gossling's shop?"

The man looked at Adele. "Don't you know you're as much meat to those mangy dogs as I am, dear lady?"

"I'm only a small businesswoman trying to make a living," Adele said. "Just like your father. So were all the people you stole from."

"But I told you, I stole nothing." His eyes snapped back to silver moons. "It was Sinbad. He's a wild animal and wild animals do what they like."

Hatfield's impatience now turned to thunder. "Where is the pen, Mr. Sipes?"

Mr. Sipes leaned back against the rough wall. "I'm sure I don't know, Sheriff."

"Are you refusing to answer, sir?" Jackson's face became opaque.

The man spit on the straw floor. "Perhaps Sinbad ate it. He's pure gold, my cat, though he's no King Midas."

"If you won't tell us here, you'll speak more plainly in a jail cell," Hatfield said. "Search his things." The young men dispersed throughout the small stall, being careful, Adele noted, not to go too near the tiger's cage.

While they did so, Adele felt her friend leave her side. Nin walked around the barn with the floating movement she recognized as the start of one of her auras.

"What is it, dear?" Adele whispered.

The woman closed her eyes. Hatfield saw her and silenced the room.

Nin's eyes flew open. "The cage. Weighed down by sparkling things."

The tiger was now alert. He had ejected little more than a lazy growl when the men entered but as Jackson neared the cage, he sprang rigid on all fours, arching his back and displaying his generous jaws. Her brother shrank back a little.

"Perhaps I ought to test your theory, Mr. Sipes," Adele said. "You said we were Sinbad's favorite acquaintances in Arrojo." She hovered next to the bars. The tiger glared but did not make a sound. "Sheriff, there's a platform of some sort underneath this."

Mr. Sipes struggled under Edison's firm grip. Adele felt around the wooden planks. A panel flew open and inside was the fountain pen, along with the other items described by the Arrojo shopkeepers, plus many other trinkets, some of which she remembered from the list. The gold pieces sparkled in the light.

"Your education didn't keep you from being a fool, sir," Jackson said. "Police in several counties have been looking for you. How did you expect to sell any of your prizes?"

"He didn't do it for the money, Jack," said Adele.

"I knew you would understand, dear lady," the man sighed. "There is no wealth in gold for me except to deplete it from others."

"I don't understand," the sheriff said.

"Don't you?" He glared at Hatfield. "More gold in my possession means less in the hands of the mangy dogs."

Hatfield motioned toward Edison and the lads. As they led Mr. Sipes out of the barn into the dark night, Adele heard him say, "How else can one break a curse but to deprive it of its worship, how else?"

~~~~~

"I can't help but wonder if Mr. Sipes didn't have a point about gold," said Hatfield the next evening. He and Lady Augusta had been invited for dinner at the Gosslings.

"The man was a raving lunatic," Jackson insisted. "He said himself gold was his curse."

The sheriff paused over his plate. "When a man's father is ruined by some material thing, whether it be liquor or dice or money, it must play in his mind like a specter."

"You always had a sympathetic heart for the most unlikely people, Horatio." Lady Augusta turned to Adele. "Even when he was a child, he would only bring home the roughest and most frightful creatures."

The sheriff blushed and fingered the large glass of wine.

"Maybe you'll explain to us now how you knew it was the cat who committed the thefts and not Mr. Sipes." Jackson glanced at his sister.

"It was really Lady Augusta who first gave me the clue," she said.

"Did I?" the elderly woman chuckled.

"Remember you said all the items that were stolen seemed small enough to fit into one's pocket?" Adele asked. "It seemed to me there was something more to it than an inconspicuous thief."

"But the cat?" Jackson asked.

"Otter stole your stickpin, didn't he?" She dabbed the gravy off her lips. "Of course, that was only a game. But it occurred to me then. Sinbad was all around my shop while Mr. Sipes was there and I paid little attention to him all the while."

"Neither did I," Lady Augusta said. "Neither did Rowena, I'm sure."

"I was more concerned about getting Mr. Sipes out than his cat," Adele continued. "Just like we were preoccupied with discussing the interviews and the suspects while Otter was there. That's how the dog could slip the pin in his mouth without our realizing it."

"Good Lord!" Jackson dropped his fork, making a dark streak on the linen tablecloth which brought Tomas, standing against the wall, to shake his head. "So that scoundrel would engage the shop owner with his nonsense while the cat stole anything it could fit into its mouth!"

"A nice bit of chicanery," the sheriff remarked.

"But how in the world would the tiger have known what was golden enough to steal?" Lady Augusta asked.

"I don't imagine it would have been difficult to train him to look for it," Hatfield said. "At Wells Fargo, we heard stories about Scotland Yard using bloodhounds to track down criminals."

"I've read tigers have excellent eyesight," Jackson said with a nod. "I suppose a golden trinket among shelves of knickknacks would stand out."

Adele fingered the lacy pattern of leaves on the gold shell of her magnifying glass as it hung around her neck. "A shame Mr. Sipes couldn't have used his college education for better purposes."

"Or more honest ones," Lady Augusta said with an arch of her brows.

When they all retired to the parlor for coffee and Jackson was showing Lady Augusta a book, she was left alone with Hatfield. "I saw the article in the *Arrojo Courier* about the thefts," she said as she offered him the box of cigars sitting on the table.

He declined. "I had a word with Miss Grace about that."

Adele leaned back. "I thought she reported the story very well."

"She left out one important fact," he said. "She never mentioned you found the stolen goods."

"Yes, I know," Adele said with a small smile.

He eyed her.

"It was at my request," she continued.

"Yours?"

"I thought with the general feeling about my involvement in criminal business —"

"Not my feeling," he said quickly. "I pushed you off this case, I know, but I realize I was wrong."

"You're generous to a fault, Sheriff," she said.

His face reddened as he played with the small spoon in the saucer. "I've always believed in giving credit where credit is due."

"And the credit is yours," she insisted. "Had anyone other than the police taken credit for catching the thief, it would have stirred the waters, and I've done enough of that for one day."

"I've never known you to back away from that particular challenge, Adele," he said with a soft smile.

"I do when it involves other people," she said. "People I admire and revere." She put her coffee cup down. "My name in the papers in connection with this affair might infuriate Mrs. Faderman and the council all over again."

"I imagine Mrs. Faderman is so well pleased the thief is in jail and the stolen items returned to their rightful owners, she would hardly be furious," he said with a smile.

"That may be, Sheriff," she said. "But it has little to do with Mrs. Faderman anymore."

"You've given this a lot of thought," he said.

She rose and wandered to the fireplace. "Ever since Mrs. Faderman came to apologize to me, I realized how very happy I am here in Arrojo. It wouldn't do to make enemies."

"Maybe not," he said. "But experience has taught me sometimes one makes enemies when one follows one's own path."

She smiled. "That may be true for a man. But a woman must be more careful."

He was silent for a moment, fiddling with the edge of his handkerchief. "Is that why the *Arrojo Courier* fingered Mrs. Faderman's dog as the key to the investigation?" He did not look at her, but his voice became sly. "I suppose a little bird told Miss Grace that?"

"Not so little," Adele said. "I thought I owed something to Mrs. Faderman after having dealt that blow to her reputation."

"You only did what you thought was right," he insisted.

"Right, Sheriff," she said, "isn't always a matter of facts. Especially when a woman values her reputation as highly as Mrs. Faderman does."

"What was it Socrates said about one's good name?"

"Regard it like a jewel," she said with a smile. "In a woman's case, she is the jewel and her reputation is the shine."

His face looked a little pale now near the lamp on the table. "Mrs. Faderman's reputation isn't your responsibility, Adele."

She sat down on the couch next to him. "I did it more for my own reputation as well as hers."

He took up the coffee cup again, though it was empty. "I don't understand."

"I know what people think of me here," she said.

"You've done nothing you need to be ashamed of," he said in a stubborn voice.

"I've involved myself in one too many crimes," she said. "In San Francisco or Sacramento, it wouldn't have been a shameful thing. But Arrojo isn't San Francisco or Sacramento."

"I'm painfully aware of that," he said with a flicker of his eyes.

"I want to live happily here," she said. "Therefore, I must be more careful in the future."

He cocked his head. "Does that mean you won't help the police anymore?"

She smiled. "I don't think I could keep from doing that, Sheriff. Not if you ask me to."

He reached a tentative hand toward hers and gave it a quick pat. It seemed all his shy nature could bear.

~~~~~

Author's Note

Hello there, reader! So you've reached the end of the fourth book of the Adele Gossling Mysteries. That's awesome! I really hope you enjoyed the story of how Adele caught a thief and his rather astounding partner in crime.

*I*f you've read the other three books in the series (and if you haven't yet, I invite you to check them out — you can get the first book for free in all online bookstores) then you'll note this book is shorter than the others. There are a few reasons for this.

*F*irst, the crime in this book is less complex than the crime of murder. Murder involves suspects, motives, and clues that go far beyond what a story of theft offers because, well, human life is at stake. Many of us view property as less involved than the taking of a human life.

*S*econd, this book was actually not originally intended to be Book 4. I wrote it in 2018 when I first thought of launching my indie author career with the Adele Gossling Mysteries (then called the Paper Chase Mysteries). I intended it to be the free book readers received when they signed up for my newsletter.

*W*hat made me change my mind? A simple question of timing. Historical fiction of any kind is unique in that time frame matters. You can read a contemporary romance, for example, where all you know is that it's contemporary, and even if the book was written five years ago, it still rings true and doesn't seem dated. But we saw more rapid developments in the past than we see today (or maybe it just seems that way).

*B*ecause of this, many historical fiction authors are deliberate in the dates they choose to set their stories because time matters. Even months can change things. For example, Book 6 of this series takes place in the winter of 1906. That might not seem like a big deal, but four months later in the San

Francisco Bay Area (where the series is set), the entire area was hit by one of the biggest earthquakes in its history and the destruction it caused was mind-boggling (which you'll see when you read Book 7 of the series).

*A*s you've seen, this book is set on Labor Day of 1904. My series begins in 1902 and there were reasons why I set the book during that year. I couldn't very well give readers a free book that was set a few years after Adele arrived in Arrojo when they might not have read Book 1 yet, right? So I put the book aside and chose something else for my free newsletter sign-up book (which you'll get a chance to pick up if you read further).

*W*hy did *The Mystery of the Golden Cat* become Book 4 of the Adele Gossling Mysteries? Again, it's a question of timing. Lionel Sipes was such a fascinating character to me, I brought him back in Book 5. Not that readers can't read Book 5 and still enjoy it. But characters build over time in a series so I wanted readers to have a chance to meet Mr. Sipes before they read Book 5 and as, at the time, Book 3 was about to launch, the only way they could meet him was if I made this book Book 4 in the series.

*H*ow about a glimpse of what's to come for Mr Sipes and the rest of the characters in Book 5 when the circus comes to town? Turn the page!

*H*appy reading!
Tam

Can Adele Gossling find out who killed a crowd-pleasing man on the flying trapeze?

The circus comes to Arrojo, an event filled with fun, enchantment, and daring at the turn of the century. The whole town is buzzing with excitement to see Julius Rowe, the Barry Circus' "man on the flying trapeze". He has looks, charm, and the enviable position of circus star. But privately, the arrogant, ambitious Julius is not much loved by his fellow performers. Except, that is, by the women. He's not above enticing wives to cheat on their husbands and get himself a few dollars in the bargain. But the crowds? They can't get enough of him!

Until one person does and kills him during his performance.

The police are baffled. Was it the husband of Julius' latest conquest? Or was it the lady herself, proving that a woman scorned can be a dangerous thing? Or was it even one of the other performers, out of jealousy and rage?

Join one of the early 20th century's clever sleuths, Adele Gossling, and her clairvoyant sidekick Nin Branch as they follow the trail of a lost scarf, a serrated knife, and misguided ambition.

Read on for an excerpt from this book!

Jackson looked annoyed, tapping his pipe on the arm of his chair. "I told Hatfield we should have run him out of town."

"I'm glad you didn't," she said. "He has some very illuminating insights into his co-performers."

"He's no performer," Jackson grunted. "He's a charlatan."

"But a very useful and observant one," she said.

He eyed her. "I'm assuming you got information out of him that might help our investigation."

"Mr. Sipes had some interesting observations about opening night."

"Oh?"

"Julius visited Calvin's wagon," Adele said.

Jackson filled his pipe with tobacco. "I'm certain many of the performers visit the man on opening night. He does take care of their salary, after all."

"I highly doubt Julius would slip into Calvin's wagon for an hour just to get his pay," Adele said dryly.

Jackson heaved a sigh and put his paper down. "All right. And why, according to the amenable Mr. Sipes, did he spend an hour in Calvin's wagon?"

"He couldn't tell me that." Adele jumped as she pricked herself with the lace needle, "But he did say the man emerged with a big grin on his face."

"Perhaps they were talking about salary after all," Jackson said. "If Calvin agreed to a substantial raise, that would cause Julius to come out grinning."

"Julius just renewed his contract a few weeks before," Adele pointed out. "One would think they would have discussed salary then."

"All right, Del, what are you really getting at?" Jackson chewed on the edge of his pipe.

"'A smile well above him,' according to Mr. Sipes," Adele added.

Jackson's eyes narrowed. "It would seem Mr. Sipes is well versed on the idea of thinking well above oneself."

"Calvin has been hiding something," Adele insisted, "something he knew about Julius that night." She rose, going over to the desk in the corner. "I found these behind the curtain." She handed him the two halves of the broken pencil.

"You think they belong to Calvin?"

"I know they do," she insisted. "It's his brand. And Cora told us he broke a pencil that night, remember?"

"What would this smug smile on Julius' face had to do with a broken pencil? It makes no sense, Del."

"I think you ought to talk to Calvin again," Adele said. "You remember his words when he saw the body, Jack? 'That wasn't supposed to happen.' Find out from him what was."

What did happen on opening night at the circus and what does a broken pencil have to do with it? I invite you to read Book 5 and find out! Copies are available at your favorite online bookstore here: https://tammayauthor.com/murder-under-a-twilight-roof-adele-gossling-mysteries-book-5 .

How about a little more of the Adele Gossling Mysteries, right here, right now? Read on for how to get hold of my free novella, *The Missing Ruby Necklace*.

FREE NOVELLA INFORMATION

When a jewel and a girl go missing on New Year's Eve...

Eleanor McCarthy, a lovely though somewhat flighty debutante, has graced the tiny town of Arrojo, California, with her presence. One of Arrojo's prominent ladies throws a New Year's Eve shindig to introduce her to Arrojo's high society — whatever little of it there is. Naturally, the daughter and son of one of San

Francisco's influential lawyers, Adele and Jackson Gossling, are invited.

But screams replace popping champagne corks when Eleanor's priceless ruby necklace is discovered missing. And soon, so is Eleanor!

In this historical cozy mystery set in the early 20th century, follow Adele Gossling, stationary store owner and amateur sleuth, and her clairvoyant sidekick Nin Branch as they search for a ruby necklace that may or may not have been stolen and a young woman who may or may not have run away.

Want to read an excerpt from this book? I got you covered! Turn the page.

"Coffee!" Miss McCarthy laughed. "Heavens, no! I haven't had my first taste of champagne yet." She flung her hand out to her brother. "Bring me a bottle of champagne, my good man."

"I don't mind," he said.

Before he could saunter out the door, Mrs. Abberton jumped up. "I'll get it."

"I really think we ought to get coffee," Mr. Abberton mumbled.

"She wants champagne," Mrs. Abberton was almost stern. "It's a celebration, after all!" She practically fled from the room.

Adele followed her and caught her arm. She spoke in a soft tone. "Mrs. Abberton, why did Miss McCarthy faint?"

"She just told you, didn't she?" The woman gave a shrill laugh. "Albert said we ought to open some windows, but it was such a windy night, I —"

"It wasn't the windows," said Adele. "Or the corset."

"Of course it was!" The woman examined some bottles on the floor. "I never could read these labels."

"You were staring at Miss McCarthy as if something that wasn't there."

"What an imagination you have, dear." The woman said.

"Miss McCarthy had her hands on her throat when she fell," Adele continued. "You kept looking at her throat."

"Nonsense," the woman hissed.

"Miss McCarthy wasn't wearing her ruby necklace," Adele declared.

Mrs. Abberton tore through a row of bottles lying on a table. One rolled onto the floor with a crack and the bubbly drink spilled across the marble. She sunk into one of the chairs. "You're too observant, Miss Gossling."

"You saw it too."

"Just before the lights went out," she said. "But Eleanor is one of those girls who gets easily flustered with her jewelry. She says it weighs her down."

"If that's true, why were you so alarmed just now?" Adele said.

"I wasn't," the woman insisted. "She locks that necklace in a box. Albert tried to persuade her to put it in our safe at the finance company, but she refused."

"That's rather unusual," Adele said.

"Eleanor's a lovely girl, but rather flighty," The woman said in a harsh tone. "I expect Celestine spoils her."

"If the necklace is missing, there might be a theft involved," Adele suggested.

Jewelry goes missing all the time. But does that mean theft? And why is Mrs. Abberton so nervous?

How can you get your hands on a copy of *The Missing Ruby Necklace*, not available in any bookstore? Simple. Go to this link: **https://landing.mailerlite.com/webforms/landing/l2u0c3.**

What else will you get when you get this novella? How about fun facts about women in history and true crime classic mysteries, which are just as fascinating, if not more so, as contemporary true crimes?

ABOUT THE AUTHOR

Writing has been Tam May's voice since the age of fourteen. She writes stories about powerful women set in the past. Her fiction gives readers a sense of justice for women, both the living and the dead. Tam's stories are set mostly around the Bay Area because she adores sourdough bread, Ghirardelli chocolate, and San Francisco history.

Tam is the author of the Adele Gossling Mysteries which take place in the early 20th century and feature sassy suffragist and epistolary expert Adele Gossling whose talent for solving crimes doesn't sit well with the ideas of some people around her about women's place. The first book of the series reached #1 in its category on both Amazon and Apple and went into the Top 100 Kindle Free Books list on Amazon for the entire store.

Tam has also written historical fiction about women defying the confinements of their era. Her post-World War II short story collection, *Lessons From My Mother's Life*, debuted at #1 in its category on Amazon, and the first book of her Gilded Age family saga, the Waxwood Series continues to remain in the top 10 in its category.

Although Tam left her heart in San Francisco, she lives in the Midwest because it's cheaper. When she's not writing, she's devouring everything classic (books, films, art, music) and concocting yummy vegan dishes.

Tam May can be reached at:

WEBSITE: http://tammayauthor.com/

EMAIL: tammay70@tammayauthor.com

FACEBOOK: https://www.facebook.com/tammayauthor

INSTAGRAM: https://www.instagram.com/tammayauthor/

PINTEREST: https://www.pinterest.com/tammayauthor/

www.ingramcontent.com/pod-product-compliance
Lightning Source LLC
Chambersburg PA
CBHW031000210726
48290CB00007B/2405